Noni raised her eyebrows. 'Even when you're obviously not normal?'

'Ha. Ha.' Iain tilted his head. 'Don't you have to get ready for classes?'

Jacinta didn't even smile as she placed her dinner plate on top of her father's. She'd been very quiet since she'd also found out Iain was a doctor.

Noni was over her shock now. 'So why did you choose surgery?'

'I really don't want to talk about it, OK?' Iain stalked off to the kitchen.

Noni frowned. What was his problem? What was wrong with her being interested?

Fiona McArthur lives with her Ambulance Officer husband and five sons in a small country town on the north coast of Australia. Fiona also works as a midwife part-time in the local hospital, facilitates antenatal classes and enjoys the company of young mothers in a teenage pregnancy group. 'I'm passionate about my midwifery and passionate about my writing—this way I'm in the happy position of being able to combine the two.'

Now that her youngest son has started school, Fiona has more time for writing and can look forward to the challenge of creating fascinating characters in exciting Medical Romances™ for her readers to enjoy.

Recent titles by the same author:

DELIVERING LOVE

MIDWIFE UNDER FIRE!

BY

FIONA McARTHUR

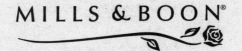

MILLS & BOON®

To my husband, my own hero.

All the characters in this book have no existence outside the imagination of the author, and have no relation whatsoever to anyone bearing the same name or names. They are not even distantly inspired by any individual known or unknown to the author, and all the incidents are pure invention.

*First published in Great Britain 2001
Harlequin Mills & Boon Limited,
Eton House, 18-24 Paradise Road, Richmond, Surrey TW9 1SR*

© Fiona McArthur 2001

ISBN 0 263 82672 4

*Set in Times Roman 10½ on 12¼ pt.
03-0601-44220*

*Printed and bound in Spain
by Litografía Rosés, S.A., Barcelona*

PROLOGUE

'JACINTA is your child. For the last seventeen years, I've managed without you—but it's different now. I'm not well and I'm worried about her.'

Iain McCloud shifted his eyes to the envelope that had carried the missive. It was crossed with address changes and the Lost Letter Office mark.

He screwed the envelope into a ball to let it fall to the carpet then lifted his fingers to massage his temples. Why had Adele not told him? He would have been there for her and the baby.

He remembered the summer it must have happened. She'd been much older than he and they'd been inseparable. Until the day Adele had changed. Was that why she'd sent him away?

What thoughtless hardship had he visited on the daughter he hadn't known?

Jacinta. She would be almost an adult now and he didn't even know what she looked like. He could have passed her in the street and known nothing.

He felt like he'd been hit with a sledgehammer. Where was she? He had to find them both. He'd make it up to them.

Unable to stand still, he strode across to the huge windows to let some air in and smashed the heel of his hand into the window-sill. He stared blindly out at the Harbour Bridge. The green Sydney ferries and even the tall ship with waves creaming off the sides passed unnoticed. He reached for his phone.

5

CHAPTER ONE

THE birth brought back so many memories. Noni Frost stood beside the bed and smiled mistily at two of her previous antenatal students. There were many things she admired in these two young women as they met each new challenge that their unplanned pregnancies threw up at them.

Kylie rested wearily back on the beanbag and hugged her baby to her breast.

Amanda, heavily pregnant, stared awed at her friend. Noni suspected that Amanda was uncomfortably aware her own labour was fast approaching. Noni made a mental note to take Amanda aside and answer any new concerns she might have now that she had witnessed Kylie's baby being born.

The new mother looked up, tired but triumphant. 'Thanks for staying, Noni. I did it. You said I would but I can't believe it.'

Noni leaned over and brushed the damp tendrils of hair from the girl's forehead.

'You were wonderful, Kylie. Congratulations on your beautiful daughter.'

She drew the other girl closer to the bed and hugged her briefly. 'You must be tired, too, Amanda, you're a great support person. Birth is pretty amazing, isn't it?'

Amanda nodded and ran her finger gently down the

baby's foot. 'Look how tiny her toes are.' She brushed a tear away from her cheek. 'I can see it's all worth it, though.'

'Definitely.' Noni smiled and tucked the bunny rug around mother and daughter as they lay skin to skin. She stepped back to check the infant was feeding correctly. Baby Sarah's little jaw moved up and down as she suckled at her mother's breast.

'I'll drop in over the weekend to see how you're getting on, Kylie, but I have to go now. You and Sarah have some time to get to know each other. Amanda will call the other midwife when you're ready to shower.'

While teaching the last antenatal class, Noni had realised neither girl had a support person to be with her during labour. The friendship she'd encouraged between Kylie and Amanda had worked beautifully so far.

She closed the door quietly and leaned back against it. Deliberately, she released a slow breath and rolled her shoulders.

Aunt Win's words to her five years ago at her own son's birth—'When it gets tough, just remember you're designed to do it,'—had been recalled to other women many times in the years between. Noni had been twenty, single and blown away by the whole birth experience, too. It would have been nice to have had a friend in the same situation there to make her feel less like a social outcast. Though there had only been the one woman who had really rubbed Harley's illegitimacy in.

She pushed herself off the door, smiling. She didn't regret a single moment with Harley.

'Hey, Noni,' Cathy called out to her from the nurses' desk. 'The supervisor wants to know if you're still here.'

Noni moved over to stare into a large box of chocolates Cathy was dividing into bags for the staff. 'Tell her I'm just going and I'm not claiming overtime.' She clasped her hands as if in prayer. 'Please, may I have mine now?'

'Poor baby. No lunch again? Have two.' She smiled down at Noni. 'They might make you grow.'

Noni poked and chose two soft-centre chocolates carefully then grinned up at the taller girl. 'Well, you'd better not have any, then.'

'*Touché.* You missed the ward meeting.' Sister Cathy Hayes handed over a copy of the minutes. 'If we lose our jobs, you might wish you had claimed overtime.'

The smile slipped from Noni's face. 'We are *not* shutting Burra Maternity Ward. There has to be an obstetrician somewhere who could settle here. The North Coast of New South Wales is supposed to be the Holiday Coast.'

'Obstetricians want cities, not towns, friend. And their wives want bright lights and private schools for their kids.' Cathy shook her head. 'It's not over yet. Dr Soams said there's a chance of a temporary guy doing emergency call for the next few weeks, but it didn't sound promising. There's another meeting with the GPs in a fortnight.'

Noni looked at her watch and grimaced. 'Damn.

OK. Have to go. I've new classes tonight and Harley's Kanga cricket training starts in twenty minutes. Kylie will give you a buzz when she's ready for a shower. Catch you later, Cath.' She grabbed her bag from her locker and took off out the door in a half-run. Harley wouldn't be happy with her.

Thank God it was Friday and she had the weekend off. The hospital had been so busy and, to make things worse, there'd recently been a baby explosion. Another of the local general practitioners had resigned and the ones left were becoming increasingly short-tempered from lack of sleep. The midwives were trying to carry the load by not calling the doctors in until absolutely necessary, but it was more stressful for everyone. They needed a permanent obstetrician desperately.

Later that evening, while she prepared the room for the new antenatal class, Noni barely heard the subtle sound of a kookaburra meld with pan flutes in the background. She rolled her shoulders and winced. The worry from reading the ward meeting minutes had caused cramps in her neck.

They had seven weeks. Dr Soams's retirement, announced today, gave them until Easter to find a new obstetrician or Burra Hospital Maternity Unit would definitely close.

She sniffed the light scent of lavender as it wafted past her towards the screen door and tried to relax.

Noni loved teaching the antenatal classes but wished she'd started the music and aromatherapy earlier. It might have helped her own first-night butter-flies.

The entrance door scraped open and she turned towards the tall, painfully thin teenager standing uncertainly in the doorway. The girl was scowling, her dark eyebrows almost meeting under the thick fringe of dark hair.

Noni made a quick calculation based on the size of the girl's stomach, and decided the young woman would be lucky to finish the classes before the baby was born. Hopefully she'd be able to have her baby at Burra before it shut. Noni clamped down on the negative thought and moved towards the newcomer.

'Hello. I'm Noni, the childbirth educator.' She smiled encouragingly and waited for the girl-woman to offer her name.

'Hello' was all she said, and pushed her protruding stomach past Noni to enter the room. She lowered herself slowly into a chair.

Not a good start. Noni blinked and turned to follow.

'I gather this is the antenatal class?' The deep, rich tones came from behind her. She was starting to feel like a clothesline twirled by children as she spun back.

This time Noni blinked for another reason. The man in front of her was older than the usual father-to-be and a good foot taller than she was. Unconsciously she straightened her spine and jutted her chin. I do not have an attitude about my height, she reminded herself.

'Yes, it is. Good evening, I'm Noni, the childbirth

educator.' She gestured towards the names in the attendance book on the table. 'If you could tick your
attendance under today's date and write your name
on the name tags for the first couple of weeks, I
should have all your names sorted out in my head by
week three.' She smiled her heck-I'm-blonde smile,
but he didn't smile back.

He ticked the last two names, Jacinta and Iain
McCloud, and the writing was firm. It didn't dare to
run out of room on the stick-on label. The guy was a
stunner but taken. She watched him position it carefully so it sat squarely on his pocket. He was also
obviously a control freak. She mentally shrugged and
turned to the next couple walking in the door.

Iain McCloud glanced at the poster on the wall of an
unborn child nestling inside a mother's uterus, and he
sighed as his gaze returned to his sullen daughter. He
couldn't see much of her mother in her, though his
memories of Adele were dim. How different his life
would have been if he'd known the consequences of
that one night!

The chairs Noni had set out formed a complete
circle around the room, even across the front white-
board, and he settled into one beside Jacinta. Very
New Age, he thought dryly. 'Try to look a little less
like you've been sentenced to the gallows, Jaz. You
might enjoy this, you know.'

I won't, he thought. This was the last place he
needed to be right now. He'd left his practice on two
days' notice for he didn't know how long. Then he'd
driven five hours to arrive at the guest house this af-

ternoon and been strong-armed in the nicest possible way by his hostess to enrol Jacinta for tonight's course. He was a city person and didn't feel comfortable in the country. What was he doing here?

Iain smiled politely at a young couple as they sat down next to them. The young man produced a small soft pillow and nestled it behind his wife's spine. Iain looked cynically towards the door to see how many more doting couples were coming. His gaze became caught by the little blonde educator.

She was running through her book and name tags spiel again and he watched the animation in her face. Her eyes and mobile mouth seemed too large for her heart-shaped face, but the more he noticed her the less he'd change. Sexy little thing, he thought, and frowned. It had been a while since a woman had sidetracked him and this was *not* the time or the place to start! He made himself look away from those perfect-sized lips and remember why he was here.

He sighed again and hoped the classes weren't going to be too airy-fairy or alternative.

'Welcome everyone. As I said when you came in, my name is Noni Frost and I'm a midwife in the maternity unit here. You all have name tags, so we'll skip the ''who I am and why I'm here'' bit.' She smiled at the sighs of relief from the room.

'Unlike school, everyone is here because they want to be.' She found herself looking up at the McCloud couple. The girl was looking down at the floor and the man was looking right back at her with a sardonic lift of one black eyebrow. *Maybe not you, buster, but we'll pretend it's true.* She looked away to the eager faces in the class.

'Tonight, we'll start with some discomforts of pregnancy and suggestions for relief your doctor may not have suggested.' The black eyebrows shot skywards. Noni ignored them.

'We call these symptoms the common complaints of pregnancy. It is useful to remember that they usually appear as a byproduct of something good your body is doing for your baby.'

Paul, a thin young man, and Suzie, his much larger wife, consulted before he put up his hand.

'What good thing is your body doing when your missus has cramps in the legs every night?' He looked around at the other men. 'She wakes up in the night and hops around the bed. I can't catch her to try and help.' The class laughed and several of the men nodded.

'Does anybody else have leg cramps?' Two of the women put up their hands and Noni smiled.

'Lack of calcium is one cause. Your baby is using up Mum's stores for itself and that's a pretty worthy cause. I'm sure you all know you can take calcium supplements, but if you increase the calcium in your food that, too, can help. More milk, fish, kelp, sesame and sunflower seeds helps, along with the dark green leafy vegetables. Other reasons are hormone changes. These prepare your body for stretching and changing shape in pregnancy and labour, so that's good for baby. Everything is more elastic, including your veins. Your body increases its blood volume and this leads to the pooling of blood in your legs. The best way to get that blood back to your heart is to use your calf muscles as the pump. So make sure you keep your calf pumps working. Rotate and work your calves when you're sitting.

'Of course, a better way is to have your man massage your legs regularly—what about it, fellas?' She smiled as the men shifted in their seats.

Jacinta McCloud looked at the man beside her and said, 'No way.'

Iain gave a short, sharp laugh and stared up at the ceiling.

Noni frowned. There was something really weird going on between these two.

There were a few smiles and strange looks from the class and Noni shifted the focus from the McClouds. 'Another good way of preventing cramps is to have a hot foot bath containing a few drops of lavender oil before bed.'

That brought Iain McCloud's eyes down from their contemplation of the ceiling. He stared at her and she could feel his attitude across the room. She knew he was going to say something. Noni sighed. There was usually at least one in every class but she wouldn't let him get to her.

'How much research has been done with oils in pregnancy? Don't you have to be careful with essential oils and the pregnant woman?' He drew the attention of the room effortlessly without raising his voice.

Noni offered a noncommittal nod. 'That's very true. Some oils are contraindicated during different stages of pregnancy and you should check with an aromatherapist if you want to blend oils during this time. Remember the concept of less is more. Lavender is safe in pregnancy if you use small amounts. The book that mentioned lavender foot baths suggested six drops—I'd suggest half that at the most. If you use too much you can reverse the response you're looking for.'

He sat back. She tagged him silently as the type to be muttering, 'Mumbo-jumbo.'

The evening passed quickly for Noni and soon eight-thirty arrived and everybody left. It was always interesting to see the way people interacted. In some groups all her jokes fell flat. This lot seemed OK except maybe for the McCloud couple. She didn't like to speculate about her clients but, heck, the girl would be beautiful if she'd only stop glaring. With his looks he didn't need to cradle-snatch either.

She didn't like him.

Iain McCloud's ideas on childbirth left a lot to be desired if the repetitive lift of his eyebrow was anything to go by. Every time she'd mentioned something about birth choices and faith in natural instincts she'd see the sceptical movement.

Maybe she was being unfair and he had a congenital twitch. She shrugged, unusually glad the class was over, and locked the last window.

It was the beginning of March and still balmy. That's what she liked about northern New South Wales—the weather and the beaches. She could do with a swim to wash away the tension from the first night. But her aunt would be waiting for her. She pulled the door shut behind her.

Tomorrow was junior cricket and her first day as coach of the under-sixes. Out of twelve boys, how come she was the only parent able to spare the time when the regular coach broke his leg?

She glanced around as she crossed the dark car park and jumped as a cat ran past her ankle. She was glad to reach her one indulgence and climb on. Noni gunned the big motorbike, grinned at the powerful response of the engine and accelerated into the corner as she left the hospital grounds.

The wind in her face blew her tension into tomorrow. It was a beautiful night and she thoroughly enjoyed the ride home. She decreased the throttle as she pulled into her driveway and the bike settled to a quieter rumble. All the lights were on in the guest house—Aunt Win's new lodgers had arrived.

Under the five-vehicle carport, a sleek Mercedes sat disdainfully next to Aunt Win's dusty tabletop utility truck. She rolled the bike over to the V-shaped ledge she'd made to save having to wrestle the bike onto its stand every night. That was the only problem when little women had big bikes. If the bike started to fall over it was hopeless.

'Noni!' Aunt Win enfolded her in her usual hug as she walked through the front entrance. A whiff of rose oil settled over her and Noni hugged her aunt back.

'You've met Iain and Jacinta McCloud, of course. They will be staying with us for the next couple of months.'

Noni tried not to gape. She should have had that

swim because it was suddenly hot in the room. 'Hello again.' Jacinta was still scowling and Noni wondered if her face got tired from holding the expression. 'Did you enjoy tonight's class?'

The girl yawned. 'Yeah, great. I'm going to bed.'

The lack of enthusiasm prickled a warning to the midwife in Noni. This young woman was in for a difficult couple of months ahead, let alone labour. She watched Jacinta pull herself up the stairs with the rail and turned back to the man beside her aunt. 'And you?'

'Very interesting.' He sounded sincere.

He had the most incredible brown laughing eyes and Noni felt an uncomfortable tug of attraction in her stomach. She'd spent the last five years clawing her way back to respectability; she wasn't about to become attracted to a married man.

'I was glad there were chairs and not the pillows and mats I was expecting.'

His smile encouraged Noni to join him in being amused. She half followed before she realised the guy was flirting with her. The slime. She stamped down any amusement, disgusted with herself for being attracted to him.

'That's week three when the physiotherapist comes. Well, nice meeting you.' Her tone said otherwise. 'I'm for bed, too.' She turned her back on him to face her aunt.

'Big day at cricket tomorrow. Harley and I should be out of here by about eight-fifteen. I'll be back before one, so you can still get away by twelve-thirty. Is that OK?'

'Fine. I'll leave a couple of quiche out and you make a salad and sweets for our guests for tea. We need to fatten Jacinta up. That girl is all baby.'

Noni laughed, her good humour restored. 'You said the same thing about me when I turned up on your doorstep.' She hugged her aunt again and nodded to Iain before half jogging up the stairs on the way to her son's bedroom.

Iain watched her tight-jeaned bottom bob up the stairs and nearly forgot to breathe. How could she do that to him just by climbing some stairs? He must be overloaded by his week from hell. He turned back to his hostess, exhaling a sigh. He'd never sleep.

'I don't often go to bed before midnight. May I use the library you showed me earlier, please, Miss Frost?'

'Call me Win, and the house is yours except for the east wing where Noni and Harley have their own quarters.'

The rosy-cheeked woman reminded him of a by-gone fairy godmother, and he mentally thanked his old mentor who'd suggested coming here for the next couple of months. He might not be a country boy, but it was true what they said about the hospitality of country people.

'Thanks, Win. I really appreciate you taking us in at such short notice.'

'Any friend of Doc Soams is a friend of mine.' She shooed him with her plump hand. 'Go through into the library and I'll get you some coffee—or would you like a glass of port?'

'Can I have both?'

She grinned at him.

'A man who charms his own way without even trying? Interesting. My niece is like that.' She chuckled as she steamed away.

He sat heavily in the big wing chair and tried to organise his thoughts. The sound as the tray was set down beside him penetrated, but he continued to stare into the empty fireplace.

'Am I the right person for her at this time? Do you think she'll ever forgive me for not knowing about her?'

There was no answer and he turned around. Ms Sexy Butt was standing there.

Iain's head jerked up. 'I'm sorry, I thought it was Win.'

'I was down in the kitchen and she asked me to bring this in. Can I help?'

He looked at the genuine concern in her face. The warmth in her eyes made him feel as if it was OK to share the burden a little. There was something about her that prevented him from erecting his usual wall of reserve and he really didn't want to be alone with his thoughts. It couldn't hurt. 'I'm worried about my daughter.'

Noni made a small sound and when he looked at her a tide of colour was creeping up her cheek. He frowned and raised an eyebrow in question.

'Um, I thought she was your wife.'

Noni felt dreadful. How could she have been so wrong about someone? She'd sensed there were undercurrents she hadn't understood between the couple. She realised she was even a little relieved. Now that, she didn't want to think about!

Noni watched Iain bite his lip and close his eyes. He opened them and grinned and it did queer things to her stomach.

'Well, thanks for the vote of confidence. You think I could entice a seventeen-year-old girl into my bed?'

'She looks older than that.'

'It's still not usually my style, though.'

'So tell me about it.'

'What? My style?'

Smart alec. 'No, I could probably work that one out for myself.'

There were those damn eyes again. Then his face changed and the humour was gone. He shrugged and gestured her to the seat opposite him.

'My wife died last year. We had no children, and I've moved house several times in the last twelve months.' His voice was flat and didn't invite sympathy so she bit back her condolences. But now she was confused. He'd said he and his wife hadn't had any children—but Jacinta was his daughter?

'Two weeks ago a letter arrived which had been following me as I moved house. It was from Jacinta's mother, Adele, who told me of my daughter's existence and asked for assistance.' The shock was in his voice.

'Naturally when I found out I hired a private investigator who finally discovered Adele was dead. Then he tracked Jacinta down.' His eyebrows drew together. 'Jacinta's mother's life was very hard from what I've gathered.' His fingers tightened around the small port glass. 'She still gave her child the surname of McCloud on the birth certificate, though. She died not long after my wife and Jacinta moved in with her boyfriend and became pregnant. When she started to show signs of pregnancy, the boyfriend left.'

He looked up. Noni winced at the expression on his face. His brows drew together again. 'I really hope I never find out who he was.' His voice was conversational but even more dangerous for that. Noni shivered in the warm night.

'So I brought Jacinta to my flat and tried to make it up to her.' He grimaced to himself at the memory.

'Last week together in Sydney was sheer hell. I couldn't say the right things, she wouldn't talk at all and I decided we'd get away in case the boyfriend found her. Somewhere I could concentrate on getting to know my daughter without my life—or, my biggest fear, her other life—intruding. The squat she was living in…' He shuddered. 'I wouldn't let a dog stay there.'

Noni almost put her hand on his knee. His distress made her ache in sympathy. She felt like a heel for her previous assumptions but he wasn't looking at her.

'Jacinta's health is run-down from poor diet and squalid living conditions, as well as the usual strains of pregnancy. I don't even think she wants to be well. It would have been very different if she'd come to me sooner. Like about seventeen years ago.'

He sighed and rubbed the back of his neck. 'Jacinta's seven months pregnant and we've a lot of cramming to do in the next two months to get to know each other. Before the third party intrudes. I'm actually becoming excited about the baby.' He laughed without humour. 'Which is lucky. Someone needs to be.'

Iain shook his head ruefully. 'So that's the story. I've got eight weeks to learn to be a father before I become a grandfather.' He seemed to shake off the despondency of his memories and fixed a teasing gaze on her.

'Now that you know I'm not a dirty old man, seducing girls young enough to be my daughter, what about you? What's your story?' His look softened and he smiled into Noni's eyes.

It was a numbing, mind-blowing smile and she felt as if she'd fallen into a wind tunnel. She forced herself to take a slow breath and feel her feet on the floor.

She was attracted to him all right. The man was like a magnet. She couldn't remember ever being as drawn to anyone before as she was to him. She tried to ignore the voice inside that suggested she go with the feeling instead of the usual back-pedalling.

She could always treat him like a holiday romance, ships passing in the night and all that. But she'd never been into that and she wasn't sure she knew the rules—if there were rules.

Then there was Harley. There'd never been a man she could trust with Harley and this one would be the same. He'd probably turn out to be another shallow man. And he was only here for eight weeks.

She could feel her heart thumping. No way! Her life was set.

'Somehow I don't think you're any sort of "old" man, and I'll reserve the rest till later. My aunt and I will help you in any way we can. Right now, I need my beauty sleep.' She spoke calmly but could feel her fingers shake. 'Goodnight.'

She backed out of the room and then spoiled it by nearly running up the stairs. She, who didn't run away from anything! Now, that was scary. He'd risen to follow her to the door and she could feel his eyes on her all the way to the top of the stairs. To look back wasn't an option.

CHAPTER TWO

THE next morning, Iain sat on the verandah with an early paper in his lap and smiled as he watched the show through the kitchen window. Family stuff he'd never been a part of. Probably would never have a part of.

Earlier, he'd jogged to the newsagents and down along the river until it reached the sea. He felt cleansed and at peace. This was a feeling he couldn't remember having had for a long time.

Maybe he *had* been working too hard the last few years. His wife, Wendy, had never stopped saying so. He winced at the ghastly time he'd had after her death. Not that it had been much better before she'd died.

He watched Noni and her son laughing at something Win said and he wondered about the boy's father. Someone else had missing links, too. Still, the boy looked happy enough.

'Come on, Harley. Can you put the kit beside the ute? I'll lift it in when I find the Thermos. There's three hours of sitting under a tree for me this morning and I'm going to need my caffeine.'

'I can't find my white shoes, Mummy.' The miniature version of Noni stood with his hands on his hips and looked at his mother.

24

'Do I wear them, mate?' His mother mimicked his stance. 'Where did you have them last?'

'Here they are.' Aunt Win came back into view with a pair of shoes in one hand and a Thermos in the other.

Both combatants smiled at her and Win turned away to fill the Thermos.

'You losing shoes is hereditary, Harley. Your mother loses everything, and I still haven't figured out how she manages to get it all back. Some guardian angel's looking after her, so you better hope they look your way, too. Now, both of you get out of here and have a good morning.'

Harley ran as fast as his little legs could carry him to get the kit from the garage, his shoelaces still undone and cricket hat having been shoved into his hand by his mother.

Win handed the Thermos to Noni. 'Here's your coffee, and here's that rulebook you said to remember. But they're only under-sixes. Kanga cricket is designed for people who don't know the rules.'

'That's lucky, then.' Noni shrugged and kissed her aunt on the cheek. 'It will be fun.' She said it staunchly but was biting her lip as she came out the door.

'Good luck.'

Noni jumped at the voice beside her on the verandah. 'Mr McCloud. I didn't see you there.'

'Iain, please. I feel like my father if you call me Mr McCloud.' He flashed one of those women-slaying smiles and Noni quelled the response that twisted up through her stomach, annoyed with herself for reacting to his charm. She wasn't in the mood.

'I wish I had time to swoon,' she mocked him, and emphasised his name deliberately, '*Iain.*'

He winced.

'But I really can't spare it.' She gave him her own version of a brilliant smile. '*Ciao.*'

He watched the tabletop truck reverse out past his car and cringed as she missed the rear bumper by a couple of centimetres. Win came out and stood beside him.

'She usually doesn't hit anything. But she comes awfully close.'

Iain just looked at her. Win dried her hands on her apron and smiled. 'I think she enjoys the challenge of taking it to the edge.'

Iain laughed. Then stopped, surprised at himself. He couldn't remember the last time he'd really laughed. He hoped this place was as good for Jacinta as it seemed to be for him.

'I've arranged an out-of-hours visit for Jacinta with Dr Soams this morning. She'll probably have to have her blood tests after that, then we'll stay out for lunch if she feels up to it. So don't worry about us until teatime.'

Win patted his shoulder. 'I won't be here when you come back, then. I spend the weekends away with friends and Noni runs the house when I have guests. Monday morning I come home early before she goes to work and I get Harley off to school now that he's started. It suits us both.' She went back into the house.

He tried to settle back to his newspaper but the

thought of Noni running the house on the weekend distracted him. He had to remember he was here for Jacinta.

Noni had a headache. She swung the ute into the garage, just missed Iain's car, and jerked to a halt. Harley was vibrant with energy and catapulted out of the car and into the house before she could ask him to carry anything in. She sighed and rested her arms on the steering-wheel to lay her head down for a few moments.

'Can I carry something for you?'

She opened her eyes and saw Iain's face peering in at her. Her head throbbed.

'How was Kanga cricket?'

'Great! I forgot my hat and had to umpire out in the sun for three hours.' Her voice was faint and seemed to be coming from a long way away. 'I think I've got sunstroke.'

Iain frowned and reached across to feel her red forehead. 'Twit. You're burning up, woman. Go inside and lie down and I'll fix the gear.' He opened the door for her and helped her out of the car.

His hand felt cool against her arm and she leaned on him for a moment while her head swam.

'You're the guest. I'll be OK.' Her voice petered out and she swayed again.

He swore and lifted her into his arms before she could protest. Then it felt too good to protest and she snuggled against his firm chest and allowed her eyes to shut. There was red light behind her eyes and she felt the nausea increasing. She prayed she could hold out until she made it to her room and concentrated on small shallow breaths, trying to keep it at bay.

Iain looked down at Noni's glowing face and decided her thick, stumpy eyelashes were more of a turn-on than long fluttering ones. She was light in his arms and he felt he could have carried her for ever, but by the time he'd made it to her bedroom at the top of the stairs he was breathing quite heavily.

So much for being a knight in shining armour. That must have been why they saved damsels in distress on horseback. He grinned to himself and laid her gently on the cover of her bed. She moaned and he remembered the only time he'd suffered from sunstroke.

He glanced around the room then tipped the contents out of a wooden fruit bowl and placed it beside her on the bed. He stood back and looked at her for a moment before heading for the door.

'I'll be back in a minute with some fluids.'

Noni felt terrible but the nausea had eased with lying down. She felt too sick to worry about being embarrassed.

'What happened to you?'

Noni forced her eyes open and squinted up at Jacinta. 'Sunstroke,' she gasped, before shutting her eyes quickly as the nausea rose again. She could hear Jacinta moving around the room and the rattle of the blinds being drawn. The darkness was heavenly and the sound of the running tap in her bathroom penetrated, but she couldn't open her eyes. A cool, wet cloth landed none too gently on her brow and she jumped, but it still felt good.

'Sorry, I didn't mean to drop it.'

''S OK,' Noni whispered. 'Feels great.'

'Iain's coming up with a drink. I'll go and talk to Harley.'

'Thanks, Jacinta.'

But the girl was gone at the sound of her father's footsteps.

Noni pulled the cloth from her eyes as he entered. Iain seemed to fill the doorway as he came through into her room, and she felt like putting the facecloth back over her face. Even feeling sick, he made her feel uncomfortably aware of him. Noni grimaced and sighed consciously to relax. He was only bringing her a drink. She forced herself up into a sitting position and took the glass he offered.

'Take your time. Little sips are often the answer. You should know that.'

Now he was talking to her like she was a three-year-old. 'I've never had sunstroke.'

'Well, what about Harley?'

As if. She was too miserable to get angry. 'I wouldn't let him get sunstroke. I make him wear a hat all the time.'

'Typical.'

She watched him raise those damn eyebrows again before he murmured, 'Don't do as I do, do as I say.'

She jerked forward on the pillows. 'Not true,' she muttered, then fell back and shut her eyes. 'If you're going to hassle me, go away.'

He smiled that irritatingly gorgeous smile and she felt her stomach clench for a different reason. She'd rather be sick.

'You look better. One more sip and I'll leave you in peace.' He slid his arm under her shoulders and flipped her pillow. He felt all solid muscle. She almost forgot to drink and wished he hadn't touched her.

When he took his arm away she missed it. Now, this was crazy. Noni leaned back on the cool pillow he'd turned, trying to re-establish her personal space and avoid his eyes. 'Thank you, Iain.'

'You sound like a polite little schoolgirl. You must be ill.' He smiled again and waved as he strode out the door.

She looked at her watch, squinting to see the hands in the dim room. One-thirty. She didn't even want to think about lunch, though. She'd have a sleep and get up at five to make the t— Her eyelids closed before the thought was complete.

It was dark in the room when Noni woke. For a moment she couldn't remember what day it was, and then it all came back. Her tongue felt stuck to the roof of her mouth and she sat up slowly to sip from the full glass beside her bed. The lemony taste loosened everything up. Even her brain. 'Hell. The tea.'

She put the glass down and swung her legs over the side of the bed. The room swung and she rocked back and forward perilously until it settled.

'That was bright,' she muttered, and looked up at a sound at the door.

'Very bright.' Iain was carrying a tray and the smell of hot quiche floated across the room to her.

'Have you got sonic ears or something?'

'Something.' He carried the tray across and set it down at the side of the bed. 'How're you feeling?'

'Better than I was this afternoon.' She looked at the tray. 'I was supposed to make the tea.'

'You can make the tea tomorrow night.'

'Yes, Doctor,' she joked, but Iain stiffened. 'What's wrong?'

'Nothing. I thought I heard Harley call.'

Noni sat up straight again. 'Harley. I have to get him his tea and make sure he has a bath.'

'Stay there!' Iain looked at her as if she were a halfwit. 'The boy is five years old. Jacinta can look after him. He knows you're not feeling well. Do you do everything for him?'

'Excuse me. I realise that with your vast experience of child-raising you know best.' Noni's hand flew to her mouth, horrified at what she'd said. Being ill was no excuse.

'That was a low blow. I'll see you later.' He left her lying there with her hand over her mouth.

'I'm sorry, Iain.' But he was gone. Well, he shouldn't have implied she spoilt Harley. No one had ever said anything detrimental about the way she raised her son. They wouldn't have wanted to.

She glared at the ceiling. Her head hurt and she didn't want the meal he'd brought up anyway.

She lay there for a while and tried to sleep. The smell of the quiche drifted around her nose. Damn him. She sat up and caught a view of herself in the mirror of the dressing-table. Frowning and glaring. It made her smile and then she realised how much of a goose she was. She'd get up and apologise as soon as she'd eaten the quiche and salad.

Jacinta and Harley were playing snakes and ladders in the library while Iain read his paper beside the fireplace. They all looked up when Noni came into the room and, strangely, she felt like an outsider in her own home. It hurt.

'You OK, Mum?'

Harley spoke from where he was sitting, and Noni quelled her disappointment that he didn't get up and cuddle her. She needed one.

'Fine, thanks, darling.' She looked at Jacinta and smiled. 'Thank you for pulling the blinds and the cool facecloth, Jacinta. It made me feel better.'

She forced herself to meet Iain's eyes. 'Thank you for looking after me, Iain.'

'You're welcome. Sit down before you fall down.'

She blinked at his tone but he was looking at his daughter.

'Jaz, would you get Noni another glass of the lemon barley water, please?'

'I'll get it.' Harley jumped up as Jacinta stood.

'You can come, too,' she said, and they both left the room.

Noni took a deep breath but before she could say anything Iain forestalled her.

'Don't apologise. I shouldn't have said what I did.'

Why didn't she feel appeased? 'Who said I was going to apologise?' She raised her eyebrows at him but had to smile at the twinkle in his eyes. 'You rat. You got me again. That's it. I'm going to apologise if it kills me. I'm very sorry for my comment, Iain. So there.'

He was still smiling. 'Very graciously offered. Now, calm down. I won't tease you any more. Did you enjoy your tea?'

She glared at him then burst out laughing. 'Yes, thank you,' she replied meekly, but the expression in her eyes warned him not to push her.

'So, tell me why you're the coach at junior cricket and nobody else could have relieved you from umpiring.'

Noni leaned back in the chair and closed her eyes. 'The usual coach broke his leg last week and is in traction in hospital. No other parent was able to take on his job so I said I would. The season's nearly finished and Harley was so excited about playing.'

'So Supermum takes on the world.'

She opened her eyes and glared.

He held up his hands and laughed. 'I'm sorry. I couldn't resist it.' He felt his forehead and rubbed it.

'What's wrong?' She leaned forward to see what was bothering him.

'Nothing. I was just checking to see if you burned a hole through my head with that last look.'

Noni quelled the urge to throw a cushion at him but felt her fists curl before she smiled. It was as if she'd known him for ever.

After one day!

She became very quiet as she sipped the drink Jacinta handed her. This was dangerous. He was a guest, and definitely a ship passing in the night.

The phone rang. 'I'll get it.' Harley bounced off

the floor and raced into the hallway. He came back. 'It's for you, Mr McCloud. It's Dr Soams.' His little voice struggled over the words.

Noni watched Iain frown as he left the room. This was interesting. Just how well did he know Dr Soams and his daughter? Penelope, a girl she'd been to school with, had been the Burra Show Society Princess the year Noni had been pregnant with Harley—and hadn't she rubbed it in. Noni sat up straight.

Harley climbed onto her lap and she cuddled him. 'You had a big day today, mate. How about you go to bed? I'll be up in a minute to see you. Say goodnight to Jacinta.'

'G'night, Jacinta. G'night, Mummy.'

She heard him say, 'G'night, Mr McCloud,' as he passed through the hall. She looked across at Jacinta.

'What did you do today?'

'We went to see Dr Soams, and that Penelope woman took some blood.'

Jacinta scowled again and Noni hid a smile behind her glass as she took a sip. 'Did it hurt?'

'Nah. But I hate needles.' She looked thoughtful. 'Lucky, I s'pose. If I hadn't I probably would have tried heroin.'

Noni choked on her drink. She started to cough and put the glass down hastily.

'Are you all right?' Jacinta jumped up, belly and all, and hovered near Noni's chair, ready to thump her on the back. Iain came through the door and stared at Noni as tears streamed down her face and she gasped for breath.

'What are you doing now?' He strode across the room and tapped her firmly between the shoulder blades until she stopped. He handed her a handkerchief from his pocket to mop up.

'Drink down the wrong way,' Noni gasped, and took another sip to soothe her throat. It started another fit of coughing but she had it under control quickly. Iain leaned towards her again. 'No. Don't help me any more. The cure is worse than the disease.'

Jacinta looked from one to the other and shrugged. 'I'm going to bed, too. See ya tomorrow.' She cast one warning look at Noni and shook her head. Don't tell my father, it said.

'See "you" tomorrow, not "ya", thanks, Jacinta,' her father corrected.

'Spare me,' she threw over her shoulder, in exactly the same tone as he'd used.

Noni tried not to laugh but couldn't help it. Of course it started the coughing again and she got up from the chair and backed away from him. She held up her hands as he advanced towards her.

'Spare me,' she spluttered.

He dropped his hands and settled sedately into his seat before fixing her with a penetrating gaze. 'What was that all about?'

'Girl talk.' Noni had her breath back now and was in a spot. She should tell him what had passed between them but it would destroy any chance of gaining Jacinta's confidence.

Iain raised one eyebrow but didn't say anything. 'Fine. I have to go out. Are you well enough now to leave in charge of the house?'

He was probably going to see Penelope Soams. He could have her. 'Perfectly fine. Don't let me cramp that style.' He didn't say anything. Just looked.

He rose from the chair and turned towards her before leaving. 'Goodnight.'

'Goodnight.' She sat in the empty room for at least another hour before heading back to her bed. She still had a headache and when she looked in the mirror her face was unattractively red. She felt like crying but it was probably from the sunstroke.

The theatre sister showed Iain into the operating theatres at Burra Hospital and he noticed her staring at him. He supposed that was how it was in a country town. New people stood out here, unlike the useful anonymity of the city. He winked at her and she looked startled. He strode over to his old mentor.

Dr Soams looked up and smiled. 'Thanks, Iain. We don't usually deliver twins here, especially if they're both breech like these little tykes.' He smiled at Iain's grim expression. 'No, I'm not just trying to trick you into liking it here. They really won't wait for the road transport to take them to the base hospital.'

Iain nodded. 'I understand that. Glad I could help. What's the story?'

'Mum's unbooked and previously undiagnosed with the twins. Silly girl's afraid of doctors and never got around to making the appointment. She lives with her partner up in the hills and they were going to have the baby at home. But he got cold feet when she went into labour, thank God. He nearly had a heart attack when I told him there were two of them.'

Iain shook his head. 'I didn't think that sort of thing happened any more. Undiagnosed twins are rare enough, but no antenatal care is criminal.' Iain followed him into the scrub room and glanced around, as if expecting more people. His eyebrows lifted. 'Just the two of us?'

Dr Soams nodded towards the window into the other theatre. 'The other two doctors are stuck in there with a fractured femur. It's damn lucky you're here or it would be the midwives, theatre sister and me. Not that we haven't done it before.'

He chuckled at Iain's resigned shake of the head. 'Welcome to obstetrics in the country. It's a bit different to the Royal, or your flash practice in Macquarie Street, eh?'

Iain pulled on his gloves. 'Quite,' he said dryly, and stepped back for the older man to precede him through the theatre door.

Dr Soams paused and looked back over his shoulder. He added slyly, 'If Noni Frost finds out you're an obstetrician your peace is gone. Determined woman at work and a good midwife. Stands up for her women and lets the GPs know if she doesn't agree with their management.'

'I won't be duelling with her. Tell them all I'm a plain surgeon if she has to know, to keep it simple. I'm going back to Sydney after Jacinta's baby is born.'

'That's right, you are, too.'

Iain didn't like the way he said that but they were finally moving into the theatre.

'We're ready to start, Beulah. Nearly time for you

to go to sleep, my dear. This is Dr McCloud—he's come to help me with the operation.'

Iain looked over the sterile drape at the two huge pools of fear that were the young mother's eyes. He tried to imagine the transition from too scared to attend a doctor's visit to an operating theatre and surgeon's knife. His voice was soft as he injected as much reassurance as possible into it.

'Hello, Beulah. I'm Iain. We'll take very special care of you and your precious babies. Go to sleep and don't worry. When you wake up it will all be over.' His eyes smiled above the mask. 'This will probably be the most rest you'll have for a while, once these two are born.' The woman half smiled and her eyelids fluttered shut.

Dr Soams manoeuvred himself into the assistant's position and Iain raised his eyebrows in amusement.

'Fine. I'll stand here. Do you want to see how good a teacher you were?'

The older man chuckled. 'You outstripped me years ago, Iain. I just want to take it easy when I can at my age.'

'You poor old thing.' Iain's eyes narrowed and he glanced at the anaesthetist before resting the scalpel on the patient's skin. His voice was different. 'Ready to go ahead.'

'She's under,' the anaesthetist agreed, and the operation began.

It took fifteen minutes for the first twin and another two minutes for the second. The theatre sister enjoyed the challenge of keeping up with the unaccustomed speed and deftness of the surgeon. Dr Soams was chuckling.

Closure was complete in thirty minutes and the theatre sister was still shaking her head as the final instrument count was completed. She couldn't wait to tell the others.

Noni saw the lights on her ceiling from Iain's car well after midnight, and for some reason the sleep that had eluded her finally drifted into place.

CHAPTER THREE

'HELLO, everyone. Welcome to week two. Tonight we are going to go through the anatomy and physiology of labour and later the dietician is going to come in and talk to you about any dietary concerns you may have.' Noni looked around the room, yet avoided looking at Iain. At least Jacinta wasn't scowling.

'After her visit we'll watch a video of a normal labour.' She smiled around the room. 'This video is set in the Netherlands and the woman has chosen to have a home birth and midwife carer. If you have the baby at home, it's under your own steam and doesn't include the option of medicated pain relief. Home birth is quite accepted practice overseas but a little harder to arrange in Australia.'

The class shifted in their seats and a few of the girls looked horrified at the thought of not having options in pain relief. Iain raised his eyebrows.

Noni passed the plastic pelvis around the room, waiting until it came back to her. She showed the little doll and explained the increased space in the pelvis for the baby to pass through if the woman was upright instead of being on the bed.

'So stay off the bed, girls.'

'What's the bed for, then?' Iain couldn't stand it any longer. She'd have people hanging off lightshades if she kept this up. She looked at him and he mistrusted her smile.

'Why, for putting your suitcase on, of course.' He looked around the circle of laughing faces and felt his own lips twitch. *Good answer, you little witch. OK, answer this.*

'I can see how squatting could help, but what about the fact that these days, in our society, we don't squat? I'm not sure how long someone could take that position.' Over to you, lady. He wasn't playing fair, with Noni unaware of his obstetrics background, but he was having fun. He couldn't believe it.

'That's why we have toilets. It's the perfect position for weak-kneed Caucasians. It's supported and everything is pointing in the right direction.'

She shifted to the edge of her seat and mimed concentration in pushing, and he couldn't help admiring her lack of self-consciousness. No way would he do something like that in front of a room full of people.

When do they get onto the bed? he wondered. 'Do you have many babies born on the toilet?'

Noni narrowed her eyes but the voice was innocent. 'No, but we do have fewer epidurals, forceps and episiotomies.'

She was tenacious. He'd give her that. Soams had warned him. He smiled to himself. When he refocussed on her voice she was off on another tangent, and he let the words drift over him as he watched the play of emotions across her face.

He'd only been here a week and he felt as if he'd known her for years. If this were Sydney, he probably wouldn't be fighting the attraction he felt for her so hard. If this were Sydney, he'd be trying to figure out how to get her into his bed.

He didn't see that much of her and she was away for well over her normal hours. Luckily she hadn't found out about his call-in to the hospital the other night, so he was spared that discussion.

She laughed at something and glanced at him. Iain had no idea what the joke was about but responded to the humour in her face.

He was a sensible man and she wasn't his type. He liked his women conservative, and aware of the rules. Not radical and naïve. Besides, he wasn't leaving the city and he didn't believe in long-distance relationships.

He wasn't getting involved. He looked at his daughter and flinched. He'd already failed two women, with the worst possible results. He didn't need another casualty on his slate. There was a lull in the classroom noise and Iain's attention focused again on Noni.

'Before we go any further, has anyone any questions they'd like to ask?'

Jacinta put up her hand as if she were in school, and Noni remembered just how young she was.

'Last week you mentioned the bag of waters and that they sometimes break before you go into labour or during labour.'

Noni nodded.

'What happens if they don't break?'

'That's a great question, Jacinta. Sometimes they don't break at all. Sometimes the doctor asks you if you want him to break your waters to help the labour along.'

Noni looked around the room. 'This is another example of informed choice.'

'Spare me.' The words were quietly spoken but Noni heard them.

Noni raised her eyebrows at Iain but he was contemplating the ceiling.

'You have a problem, Iain?'

'No.' The answer was short and implacable. So she ignored him.

'A midwifery tutor told me, "The membranes are baby's best protection before he or she meets their mother." I believe intact membranes often mean a slower, gentler labour as the fluid wedge of membranes against the cervix lessens the pain of dilatation. So think about it if someone suggests it would be quicker if your waters were broken.'

Iain frowned but didn't say anything.

Noni went on, 'Rarely is the baby born while the sac stays intact, keeping in mind that a baby will not open its glottis—that is breathe—until exposed to air pressure, and the mother or midwife would break the membrane to allow the baby to start life outside the womb. The old wives' tale is that any baby born with the caul over its head will never drown. In the old days midwives used to save and dry cauls and sell them to sailors to keep on their person while at sea.'

Iain rolled his eyes. 'And they wondered why people burnt them as witches.'

The men in the class chuckled at Iain's comment.

Noni let them have their laugh, secure in her own beliefs.

She smiled at Jacinta. 'Another one of my hobby-horses, I'm afraid, Jaz. Let's get on.'

The class went well and Jacinta asked another two perceptive questions about labour. Iain was being a pain, but for Noni there was a certain excitement in keeping ahead of him. He obviously knew a bit about childbirth but she could handle him. Noni was feeling quite positive about the group as she closed the windows at the end.

'We'll wait to see you lock up before we leave.' Iain's voice made her jump and she turned around slowly to face him.

'Thanks, but I'm fine. I do it every week.'

'I'm sure you do. We'll wait nonetheless.' He turned and stalked out into the foyer.

'Arrogant man.' She slammed the next window down and flicked the lock across. *What does he think I am? Some wimp afraid of the dark?* The logical side of her brain disagreed. *What are you getting so uptight about? You know you hate it when the lights are out and you have to walk across the deserted parking area.* She turned off the fan and had a last glance around the room.

They were waiting outside for her. 'Thank you.' *That didn't sound gracious,* she chided herself. Jacinta scowled at her and she scowled back.

Iain smiled. 'Well, that was fun. Goodnight.'

'Smart alec,' she muttered. Then she heard his voice drift back across the parking area.

'I have sonic ears.'

Noni gunned the motor on the bike and decided to go for a swim. She carried one of those tiny chamois towels in her bag and she could swim in her underwear. A month ago it would have been light at this time but she wasn't afraid of the dark.

The beach was deserted. Now that she was there, she really didn't want to go in, but the demon of contrariness called her. When she slipped out of her jeans and put her toe in the water she started to think of all those *Jaws*-type movies. This was dumb.

Noni pulled her jeans back on and walked back to the bike. Why should it matter if Iain was an irritating man? She climbed back onto her bike. It started to tip sideways in the uneven gutter—an inevitable slide. She strained and held it for a moment but knew it was a losing battle. She had to pull her leg out of the way smartly before it was caught underneath. Hell.

Noni swore again and reached over to switch the petrol off. She sat down beside her bike on the edge of the gutter, well aware from past experience that the bike was too heavy for her to lift once it lay on its side. She reached for her mobile phone. Aunt Win insisted she have one. Good old Aunt Win.

'Hi, Aunt. I'm fine. Is Iain there?' She listened for a moment. 'Oh. Penelope is there? No. It's fine. Don't worry.' There was the sound of voices and then Iain's voice came on.

'Where are you?'

She lay back on the grass beside the road with the phone beside her ear. 'At the main beach.' She moved the phone away from her ear as he raised his voice. When he stopped she put it back.

'No, I wasn't swimming. If you aren't too busy, could you come and help me lift my bike up?' She moved the phone away from her ear again as the volume increased. Her lips twitched.

'No, I haven't had an accident. I didn't put the stand up properly and it fell over. I'm not strong enough to lift it back up.' Her grin faded and she pulled the phone away from her ear and glared at it.

'Don't call me Superwoman and don't bother coming. I'll ring someone else.' She jabbed the talk button to cut him off.

It took him four minutes to get there. With Machiavellian nastiness he'd brought Penelope. Round one to him.

'Oh, dear, Noni.' Penelope, immaculately groomed as usual, was all saccharine and good sense. 'I always thought that bike was too dangerous for a woman. You really should get a sensible vehicle.'

Iain said nothing and Noni gritted her teeth. He strode over to the bike and reached down.

Both women watched Iain easily stand the bike up, the muscles in his arms hardening as if accustomed to the application of weights. Both raised their eyebrows and their eyes clashed.

'Noni is lucky she had you to call, Iain.'

'Mmm.' He looked at Noni from under his brows and she was sure there was some amusement there. She picked up her helmet.

Noni nodded and smiled sweetly at Penelope's sympathy. 'Thank you for lifting my bike, Iain.' Noni was trying to be very polite. 'I'll see you at home, then.' She pulled the helmet on and started the bike. Then snarled bad words all the way home.

The rest of the week continued in the same vein. Petty irritations, a very busy time on the ward and the uneasiness she seemed to feel whenever she was near Iain McCloud. She didn't feel her usual calm and competent self.

Noni tried to see as little of the lodgers between shifts as she could. Jacinta became less prickly and the first seed of trust and friendship between the two began to sprout. Noni was quite happy to proceed at the younger girl's pace.

To Iain, she was very polite.

On Friday, after handing over to the new shift, Noni overheard one of the young doctors, who had three small children, speaking to the charge sister.

'Emergency call relief isn't enough. We need another qualified obstetrician full time. I can't carry this load and my practice downtown and be human to my family much longer. I'm out of here if there's no change by Easter. I know one other guy feels the same. The hospital had better step up their advertisements or they'll have to shut the unit.'

Noni listened with deepening despair. They had a wonderful unit, caring midwives and doctors, and they provided a marvellous service to the community. To imagine all the women having to go away to the local base hospital to have their babies would be tragic, let alone the financial hardship on relatives travelling the hundred kilometres each way. There *had* to be a way to keep Burra Maternity Ward open.

She roared into the driveway after work and she could see Iain out in the yard, bowling a cricket ball to Harley. That was good of him. She craned her neck to see the shot her son played.

Noni jammed the bike into its slot, glanced at the time grimly, but stopped to lean against the side of the house to observe anyway. Harley was concentrating fiercely and Noni could see his little tongue poking out as he watched the flight of the ball. Whack. It went sailing over Iain's head and landed in the fishpond.

Harley was whooping with pride and Iain went over and clapped him on the back. They had their heads together and Noni suddenly felt left out. Maybe it didn't matter how hard she tried. Maybe Harley needed a dad to do boy things with. Men's business.

'It hurts when someone lets you down, you know.' Jacinta had come up behind her and Noni turned slowly around to face her. She knew the girl would be scowling.

She was. 'Don't trust him,' Jacinta continued. 'My mother trusted him. He let my mother and me down, and he'll let you and Harley down. He wasn't there playing with me when I was five like Harley.' She looked Noni in the eye. 'We'll be gone soon. A month and a half.'

Noni ached for the woman-child in front of her and ached for herself for what might have been. 'He didn't know you existed. How could he have come if he didn't know?'

'My mother should have gone to see him. She should have forced him to acknowledge me. Then she died and left me, too.' Jacinta's voice cracked and she moved hurriedly away.

Noni turned to follow her but just then Harley saw her and called out.

'Did you see that, Mummy? Did you see how far I hit it? Iain—I mean Mr McCloud—has been showing me how to stand and the way to hold my bat.'

Noni sent one more glance after the distant figure of Jacinta and faced the two males coming towards her. The girl wouldn't thank her if she drew attention to her tears. 'Terrific shot, Harley.'

'Mr McCloud said he'd come and help coach the team if you wanted him to.'

Iain looked sheepish as he came towards her. And so he should! She may not have been first choice for coach but at least she had stepped forward when no one else had. It hurt.

'That wasn't very diplomatic, Harley.' Iain gave her a searching look.

'What's dip-lo-mat-ic?' The boy looked from one adult to the other.

'What you're not. Now, skip inside while I talk nicely to your mother and tell her she really is a good coach.'

Harley still looked confused but did as he was told.

'I'm sorry. I didn't mean to imply you weren't a good coach.'

'Drop it. I'm tired and I've got classes tonight. Tell

them at cricket I couldn't make it and you came in my place. Controlling ten five- and six-year-old boys is much harder than managing one. You'd be doing me a favour.'

It was only half a lie. She really was tired and he would be a better coach than she was. She left him standing, staring after her, and she trailed up the stairs more depressed than she could remember.

'Hi, everybody. Welcome to week three. Is it my imagination or are all the women in this room getting bigger?' Everybody laughed and the girls patted their stomachs, even Jacinta.

'Tonight the topic is "Pain, Power and Progress in Labour." Most of the women winced.

She handed out some sheets and then pointed to a poster taped to the board.

'As you can see, this lady's smiley face is happy because she's started labour. You can tell by the contractions—the small, spaced hills drawn underneath her. She's in early labour. The contractions are probably five to ten minutes apart. This is a really good time to stay home and keep busy. Lean on the kitchen sink when you have to.' She put her hands on her hips and rocked from side to side, before going on, 'And potter around to keep relaxed.'

She pointed to the diagram again. 'Now, this next lady is looking a little less amused and her hills are closer together and a lot steeper—probably about three to five minutes apart. She's really concentrating and her mouth is a straight line. She needs to be in the shower, with her man rubbing her back. Or she could try sitting on an exercise ball, concentrating on a spot on the wall.'

She rolled a big blue ball out from the side of the room, sat on it and rolled gently from side to side on it as if she had a contraction. The class started to giggle. She got up and pushed the ball to Jacinta to try.

Iain's eyebrows were crinkled in disbelief. 'It doesn't look safe to me. What if she falls off?'

Jacinta straddled the ball and it glued itself to the floor as the base of it flattened. Noni helped her to stand up again.

'It's OK, Iain. You can have a go in a minute.' She glanced around the room. 'It's called a birthing ball and the manufacturer assures us you can use it in the shower, too. It encourages terrific positioning of your pelvis and gives your legs a rest from standing up.'

The ball moved on to Iain.

'No, thank you.'

'Wimp,' Noni said under her breath. After the ball had gone around the group she went on.

'Our third lady is looking decidedly unamused. Her contractions are close together, very steep and sometimes they even double up. Two to three minutes apart. That's from the start of one contraction to the start of the next. She's not getting much rest between them. She's in strong labour and almost ready to abuse her partner if he says or does the wrong thing.'

The men laughed. The women were quiet. She smiled reassuringly.

'This is all normal. One of the objects of antenatal classes is to learn different techniques to help you stay relaxed and loose, to allow these contractions to do their job as efficiently as possible. And help you recognise where you are in your labour.'

She pointed to a poster with women walking, sitting, lying over a beanbag and even squatting.

'A lot of the time, medicated pain relief can actually make your labour slower and still not give you the type of relief you want. That relief will come when you have your baby in your arms.'

Iain listened and frowned. This was too much.

'That's a bit airy-fairy for me. If a woman is in pain, and you give her something to help her, isn't it going to make her more relaxed, and speed her labour—not slow her down?' He'd had enough of this 'natural, medication-free birth' stuff. She was advocating agony when it wasn't necessary. How to make his point without sounding like an obstetrician? He chose his words carefully.

'I thought lots of women, especially first-time mothers, had epidurals. They have no pain, converse normally, even brush their hair while the labour progresses. I really can't see anything wrong with such a civilised progression.' He knew he shouldn't comment but he couldn't help himself.

Noni was looking at him as if he'd grown two heads.

'Sometimes it can help, yes.' She glanced around the room. 'Sometimes it is absolutely essential for a woman to have adequate pain relief. But the doctor's answer to pain relief isn't the only way.'

He could see the zeal. Her face became earnest and

he had to resist the urge to roll his eyes as she went on.

'Don't forget, women are designed to have babies, were born to do it, and at least eight out of ten are capable of having an active, normal labour. If somebody doesn't force an epidural down our throat or bomb us right out on pethidine. While the pain relief is there, so are the risks that are associated with any intervention.'

She gentled her voice and looked around at the women. 'You have to be careful that the reason you are having pain relief is because you need it, and not just because your partner or doctor would feel more comfortable if you'd stop groaning.'

She paused and included the men in her glance around the room this time, then smiled ruefully. 'Gee, can you tell this is a favourite lecture of mine?' The class smiled with her and the tension decreased in the room.

'We'll discuss this again and there's also a night when Dr Soams comes in and explains the pros and cons of medicated pain relief.'

Iain sat back. He was an idiot for going into it now. It was all talk anyway.

He shivered suddenly at a vision of his daughter, staring up at him in pain during childbirth. One thing was for sure—Jacinta would get all the pain relief she needed, and nobody would stop him.

Noni became aware that Jacinta's usual scowl had turned into a frozen mask. 'We might just stop here and have the break now.'

Conversations broke out and people stood and

stretched before they filed out of the room to make a cup of tea. Noni went over to sit next to Jacinta. Iain was talking softly to her but wasn't getting much response.

'Can I have a go, please, Iain? Perhaps you'd leave us for a couple of minutes while I talk to Jacinta?' She could see he didn't want to go but she nudged him on his way with her hand.

When he had gone she crouched down in front of the girl. 'There's something wrong here, isn't there, Jacinta? Something big you haven't told us.' She waited and after a few moments Jacinta looked up, her eyes filled with tears.

'I know I'm going to die when I have my baby. I don't want to die and I'm scared.'

'Oh, sweetie. You're not going to die. It hurts and it takes what seems like a long time while you're having it. But then you have your baby and you know it's all worth it.'

She squeezed Jacinta's hand again. 'I think you should go home with your dad now and I'll come and see you when I finish here. OK?'

'Will you come straight home?'

'As long as I don't drop my bike, I will.' She got a small smile for that one and saw Iain hovering at the door. She gestured him in. 'I think you should take Jacinta home now, Iain.'

He searched her face and that was enough for him to help his daughter to her feet without saying anything.

She watched them go and pulled her mind back to the class. The physiotherapist would be here soon and she needed to set up the mats for the session on exercises in pregnancy. The next hour seemed to drag while she worried about Jacinta. She was glad she didn't have to be responsible for this lesson. Finally the physio wound up her talk and Noni thanked her for coming. It was time for home.

'Don't forget to meet at the steps of the maternity unit next week. We're doing our birthing unit tour and we won't come to this room at all.'

'She's asleep.' Iain was waiting for her as she came through the door.

Noni looked at his strained face. 'Did Jacinta tell you she's scared of dying in labour?'

He seemed to look through her for a moment and then refocus.

'So that's it. Every time I think I'm getting to know her I realise how much I still have to find out. I'm running out of time before the baby is born. Adele should have told me about Jacinta when she first found out she was pregnant.'

'Oh, great. Blame the poor woman who was probably scared and not sure of her reception from you. For all you know, she might have been trying to find you for years.'

Noni felt like stomping her foot.

She fell back on her midwifery training. 'Important fears and significant events in her life that we know nothing about are going to make a difference when she goes into labour.'

Iain ran his hand distractedly through his hair. 'I'm getting eighteen years of grey hairs in two months.'

Noni tilted her head. 'And very becoming it is, too. Forget the cricket tomorrow. I'll take the kit and umpire.'

His laugh was harsh. Not like him at all. 'No, I'll go. I'll need something to take my mind off all this. Would you stay home with Jacinta?'

'I think that's a great idea.' She rubbed her eyes. 'I have to go to bed. It's been a big week at work again. Everything seems to be going wrong at the moment.'

He looked at her as if he was going to say something and then changed his mind. She'd hoped he'd listen to her work problems but she couldn't understand why she'd thought he would. He was just a temporary lodger after all.

'See you tomorrow.' She turned away, but before she reached the stairs she heard his voice.

'Thank you, Noni. I couldn't have handled it without you.'

She sighed and whispered, so he wouldn't hear, 'Yes, you would have.'

She trod the stairs and his voice floated up. 'No, I wouldn't, and I've still got sonic ears. By the way, I'm not a wimp.'

Of course they won at cricket. And she hadn't seen it. Harley came through the door as if he'd been fast-bowled towards her.

'You should have been there, Mummy. We won and I hit a four!'

Noni looked at his little face, glowing with excitement—or was that sunburn? 'Did you have your hat on?' She touched the heat on his face.

'Mummy? I said I hit a four.' Her son was frowning. Here she was, thinking about whether Iain had looked after her son well enough!

'I'm sorry, darling. That's wonderful news. I was just feeling sorry for myself 'cause I didn't get to see you hit a four.' She hugged him but he wriggled away like a fish to hop around the room in his excitement. 'Tell me all about it.'

'Harley!' Iain's voice came in from the carport. 'Come on, mate. Bring some stuff in from the car.'

'Gotta go.'

Noni frowned as he raced out the door to do as Iain told him. There was that pain in her heart again.

'How's Jacinta?'

Noni looked up at Iain and glared at him. 'Your daughter is fine and my son is sunburnt.'

Iain frowned and didn't say anything for a moment. 'Is that really the issue or are we working on another level here?'

Noni stared at him. She felt the weight of tension in her shoulders. The rat. How did he know that? She turned her back on him. 'Aunt Win's gone and Jacinta is in the lounge. It's good news the team won.'

He came up behind her and she felt him even before they touched. Then his body was right up against her back, warm and solid. She tried to stay rigid but he felt so damn good. It would be nice to have someone to lean on once in a while—as long as she remembered he was just being kind.

She leaned the back of her head on his chest and

strong arms came around her. Slowly he turned her around and she buried her nose in his chest as he smoothed the hair back from her forehead. The scent of his body and some woodsy cologne proved a heady mixture, and she closed her eyes to savour it.

'You needed a hug, didn't you?' His chest vibrated as he spoke, and she buzzed as if she'd plugged herself into an energy source. A minute ago she could hardly lift her feet and now she was starting to feel better. Even her sense of humour was recovering.

'Yes. I did,' she mumbled into his shirt, but still neither of them moved.

'What are you doing?' Harley's voice intruded and Noni tried to pull away, but Iain held her firmly against him.

'Your mummy needed a hug, just like you need a hug sometimes. We'll have to make sure she gets more. All right, mate?'

'Oh. OK,' he said. 'Can I play on the PlayStation?'

Noni was having trouble containing her giggles. 'Uh-huh.' She nodded her head. 'How long does this hug therapy last?'

'Bored already, woman?' He slid his finger under her chin and tipped her face up.

Noni frowned. 'Your face seems so far away up there in the air. You're too tall for me.'

He brought his face lower. 'Is this better?' His lips were only a few centimetres from hers.

'What are you doing?' Jacinta's voice interrupted them, and this time it was Iain who tried to pull away. Noni held onto him as hard as she could, and after the first resistance he stayed where he was.

'Your father needed a hug. Just like you need a hug sometimes. We'll have to make sure he gets more. OK, Jacinta?'

'Yeah, right. Spare me.' But she wasn't frowning as she left the room.

'Cheeky little thing, aren't you?' Iain pretended to glare at her.

Noni was feeling quite pleased with herself. She smirked. So he kissed her.

His lips came down on hers like a down quilt. Soft and light and deliciously warm. She found herself stretching up on tiptoe to try and get closer to him. His breath mingled with hers, and if they did much more of this she could forget about the room, Harley and Jacinta, how organised and set her life was, Penelope... She pulled away. She'd almost forgotten.

'Penelope rang. She wants you to ring her back.' She watched him open and shut his eyes slowly.

'That good, eh? My technique is definitely slipping.' He glared at her. 'You are *not* supposed to remember phone messages when I'm kissing you!'

'I *nearly* forgot about the message.' She grinned up at him. 'It'll do you good. You're too cocksure of yourself anyway.' She stepped out of his arms, suddenly full of energy, and moved over to the fridge. 'I think I'll make something super for tea tonight.'

She heard him mutter as he left the room, 'That would be appropriate, for Superwoman.' She had to smile.

Later that evening, Jacinta and Noni dragged the old sewing machine out. Both sat on the carpet, staring at the inside of the machine. They had planned on hemming some baby-print flannelette sheeting they'd bought for bunny rugs, but couldn't get the machine to work. Neither of them had ever had much to do with sewing machines.

Jacinta was fed up with trying to decipher the book. 'Get Iain to have a look at it. Men are supposed to be able to do things like this.'

Noni frowned. 'I hate that sort of mentality. There's no reason why I haven't as much chance of figuring this out as your father. Unless he's a sewing-machine mechanic, which I very much doubt.' She looked up from peering inside the machine. 'What does he do?'

'I don't think he does anything. He certainly hasn't been to work since I've known him. I never asked him.'

Noni's eyebrows drew together again. 'Do you ever ask him anything? Aren't you curious about him?'

Jacinta shrugged and Noni tried again.

'Look at it from his point of view. Finding you was a huge change in his life. I think he's adjusting pretty well.'

Jacinta scowled. 'You're just saying that because he hugged you. You're on his side. I don't want to make your stupid bunny rugs anyway.' She threw the book at the machine and climbed slowly to her feet, before waddling out of the room.

'Good one, Noni.' She sighed.

'What's a good one?' Iain spoke from the doorway as he watched his daughter pull herself up the stairs. Then he came into the room.

'Nothing, Big Ears. Are you a sewing-machine mechanic?'

'No, but men are supposed to be able to figure these things out. Hand me the book.'

'Great, it's hereditary. Your daughter said that, too.' She threw him the book. Noni watched his bent head as he tried to follow the diagrams, compared to the real thing. It really was a very nicely shaped head.

'So, what do you do?' she asked to distract her eyes.

Iain looked up warily. 'What do you mean, what do I do?'

'Your job, profession.'

'Oh.' He remembered Soams's warning about telling Noni he was an obstetrician. His gaze fell on the newspaper on the chair. 'I'm a stockbroker.' It wasn't a lie really. He had shares left by his grandfather, although he didn't actually buy and sell them. Still, he checked on them most days for the heck of it.

Noni frowned and then slowly nodded. 'OK. So you just left work when you found Jacinta and nobody minded?'

'Plenty of people minded, but it was something I had to do. You probably guessed that money isn't a real problem. Actually, I'm enjoying the first holiday, if that's what you can call it, in a lot of years.' He had a sudden thought. 'I took three months' leave and I've had over a month now. I'll be a grandfather in five weeks if the baby comes on time.' He looked across at Noni, horrified.

Strange sounds were coming from behind the hand over her mouth.

Iain winced. 'It's not funny. I'm thirty-nine years old, and I'll be a grandfather.'

'Would you like me to get you some hot milk?' Iain glared at her and snorted in disgust when she fell over on her back with the giggles.

She looked like a deliciously cheeky elf and he wanted to kiss her. Wanted to breathe that flowery scent of hers that was starting to drive him a little wild every time he came near her. But he had to keep it light.

He advanced towards her on all fours and planted his hands on the carpet on either side of her head. 'Stop your unseemly mirth, woman.'

She looked up and he noticed that dark green ring around her corneas. Her eyes were really quite beautiful.

Noni stared back at him. He was so close she could feel the heat of him and he made her feel brave and audacious.

'Your grandchild will be gorgeous. And you don't look too bad for your age.' She reached up and put her arms around his neck and he lowered his face until they almost touched. 'Come down here a bit closer—you're always towering over me.'

He stared into her eyes. 'I think you have the sexiest eyelashes I have ever seen.'

She smiled, tingling with the unaccustomed sensations he seemed to ignite in her. 'Idiot. I have short, stumpy eyelashes. Sexy is long and sweeping, like a giraffe.'

'No. Seriously.'

'Right. Seriously. Sure, this is serious, just kiss

me.' She could feel her new-found bravado draining away and she tried to hold onto it.

'No. This is important. Your eyelashes are like you.'

He really was only playing with her. He probably didn't find her attractive at all. Noni rolled away.

'Great. I'm short and stumpy. Thank you!' She glared at him. 'How to ruin a mood in three easy steps.'

'Ho-ho.' He glared back. 'Who remembered a phone message during our memorable first kiss?'

She tilted her head. 'How is the delectable, giraffe-lashed Penelope?'

'Jealous, are you?' He smirked.

'Drop dead. You...*stockbroker*.' She got to her feet. 'I'm out of here.' She pointed to the machine. 'Fix the sewing machine for your daughter. Men can do that. Remember?'

Iain watched her leave the room. Flounced, he thought to himself. He wasn't quite sure what had happened there, but it hadn't been boring. Had he done the right thing, saying he was a stockbroker? He really didn't want to discuss hospitals and obstetric staff shortages when he wouldn't be staying in the area. So much for the resolution about not getting involved. His mood lightened.

She obviously didn't like it when Penelope rang him. He must get her to ring more often. He had a whole day tomorrow before Win came home to chaperon.

CHAPTER FOUR

AMANDA went into labour early on Thursday morning. When Noni entered the birthing suite, the young girl was sprawled across a beanbag while Kylie rolled the wheeled massager rhythmically over her back. The contraction finished and Kylie reminded her friend to sigh after the pain.

'You ladies look great. Night Sister said you started labour at three and came in at six this morning, Amanda. You did well to stay at home that long on your own.' Noni crouched down beside her and rested her hand on the young woman's shoulder. 'How're you going now?'

'I'm OK. I knew you'd be here soon. I rang Kylie and she was here to be with me.'

Noni laughed. 'At least we don't have to worry about babysitters for Kylie's baby. In between feeds the nursery staff will watch her for us. We'll just push Kylie out the door when her baby needs feeding.'

She pulled a footstool over to the beanbag and settled herself onto it. 'So, can I have a listen to your baby, please, Amanda?' Noni pulled the portable Sonicaid out of her pocket and squirted some clear jelly on the end.

Amanda pulled up her T-shirt and shifted to allow Noni to rest the small, torch-shaped Foetal Doppler against her stomach. The steady clop, clop, clop of the baby's heartbeat brought a smile to each face. 'Baby's happy. How're you feeling in yourself, Amanda?'

'Excited.' She grimaced. 'Scared.' A look of resignation appeared on her face as a contraction quickly built. She breathed, Kylie rubbed and Noni soothed.

By three o'clock in the afternoon Amanda's contractions, despite being regular and strong, seemed to be taking too long to progress her labour. The baby's head wasn't moving down into Amanda's pelvis as Noni would have liked.

'How much longer?' Amanda's voice was agitated and Noni sponged her face with a cool, damp cloth.

'It's OK, sweetheart. You're doing beautifully. Do you want to go back in the shower?'

'We've tried everywhere, Noni. Nothing seems to work. I'm so tired.'

'You're certainly giving everything you've got, Amanda.' Noni frowned and some deep instinct rattled alarm bells of premonition. She reached for the blood-pressure cuff.

'Your blood pressure is climbing a little, Amanda.' She packed that away and pulled the Foetal Doppler from her pocket. They all listened to Baby's heart rate and even Amanda managed a weak grin. 'I'll just dash out to the desk and give Dr Soams a ring to keep him up to date with your progress.'

'I thought I wasn't making any progress.' Amanda's mouth curved in a tired smile.

Noni leaned over and brushed the damp hair back from Amanda's eyes and smiled back. 'Things are always changing. No contraction is wasted.'

As she walked up the corridor Noni was frowning.

'Problems, Noni?' Cathy looked up from the report she was writing before going home.

'The head's just floating around the brim of the pelvis. She's dilated about seven centimetres and I've got goose-bumps.'

Cathy looked up sharply. 'I hate it when you do that.'

Noni grimaced. 'Yeah, so do I.'

'I'll phone Aunt Win to say I don't know when I'll be home, and try Dr Soams's number again.' She put the phone down a minute later.

'He's still at the base hospital for the meeting. Can you page one of the other GPs to come and assess the situation? I'll go back in.'

As soon as she opened the door she knew something was wrong.

'Noni! My waters broke and what's that?' Amanda's wail coincided with Kylie's frightened cry.

A thick purple coil of shiny umbilical cord pulsated between Amanda's legs, and Noni felt her stomach drop into her lace-up blue shoes. Cord prolapse!

'Kylie, hit the red buzzer a couple of times, please, and the other midwife will come in.' She threw a thin pillow onto the bed. 'OK, Amanda. Things are going to happen really fast for the next ten minutes so I'll explain as we go along. Up on the bed on your hands and knees with your bottom in the air, my love. Almost bury your face in the pillow. We have to get gravity to keep your baby's head from leaning on the cord.' It was easier said than done but Amanda didn't complain.

'You and I are going to get *real close* for the next ten minutes. Cord prolapse means that, instead of the head coming first, a loop of cord flopped in front of it when your waters broke. So the cord came right out. Babies don't like this and need to be born as soon as possible. This means a Caesarean, hopefully in the next ten minutes.'

'Will my baby be all right?'

'The sooner we get you to the theatre the better.'

Cathy skidded to a halt as she came in.

'Cord prolapse.' Noni didn't need to elaborate.

'Both obstetric GPs are in Theatre in the middle of a case. They'll be another hour.'

'An hour's no good for us. Ring the supervisor and tell her we don't have time to hunt. Get someone now—a surgeon, anyone—and we'll prep Amanda for Theatre.'

Three minutes later. 'Very tricky, this,' Noni mumbled as she taped the catheter to Amanda's leg. 'How're you holding up, sweetheart?'

'I'm scared.' Amanda was shaved, changed, prepped for Caesarean section and shifted onto the emergency trolley for transport to theatre. All done upside down with Amanda in the knee-to-chest position.

They whooshed through the theatre doors.

Theatre Sister was as quick as she could safely be. 'What's your name? Show me your armband. Which operation are you having?'

Amanda mumbled the answers and Noni hurriedly completed the notes as the trolley burst through the second set of doors.

'I'll be there in a minute, Amanda.' Noni turned and sped into the change room to don her theatre scrubs and mask.

When she made her way to Theatre One, Amanda had been shifted to the table and onto her back to allow the anaesthetist to do his work. Noni slipped her hand into Amanda's and squeezed. 'I'm right here and will be with you when you wake up.'

'I'm so scared for my baby, Noni.'

'I know, sweetheart. Think lots of strong, positive vibes as you go to sleep and your baby will know.'

She watched the girl's eyelids flutter and the cold hand in hers loosened as Amanda became unconscious.

The scrub room door burst open as the surgeon strode into the room with his gloved hands clasped in front of him. There was something familiar about the set of the shoulders and the carriage of his head before Noni noticed his eyes.

She'd said 'anyone'. She hadn't meant Iain!

Iain nodded grimly at her. 'Yes, I'm a surgeon. They couldn't find an assistant, so you'd better get scrubbed, Sister. They've rung for another midwife to resuscitate the baby.' Then he ignored her as he and Theatre Sister began the skin prep and draping procedure.

Noni shook her head once as if to make the reality of Iain being a doctor soak into her numbed mind. Then she pushed it aside and concentrated on getting to the scrub sink and back as efficiently as she could. Every second counted for Amanda's baby. Her head shook as she scrubbed away and she couldn't help but mutter as she washed. He'd said he was a *stock-broker*!

When she stepped up opposite him, Noni couldn't believe her eyes. Any lingering doubt that Iain was a skilled surgeon was banished for ever.

She took over holding the retractor and received a grateful glance from the scrub sister, who'd been doing two jobs. 'You don't need an assistant. You and Sister are almost at the uterus already.'

'Hold the sucker,' Iain said. 'I'm ready to pierce the membranes. There's not much movement here from Baby but there might be enough.'

The raucous sound of the suction removing the sudden gush of green-tinged fluid filled the theatre. She had expected that sign of foetal distress and hoped none of the soiled fluid would be inhaled into the baby's lungs. Noni held her breath for the last few seconds as Iain slipped his hand inside the uterus. He dexterously slid the baby's head out through the opening, unravelled a loop of cord from around its neck, then quickly drew out the limp, blue body of a baby girl.

Noni slipped the tiny suction tube into the baby's mouth in case she took her first breath with a mouth full of the green fluid. The cord was clamped and cut and the baby handed swiftly over to the other midwife standing beside the table with a sterile drape over her arms.

Noni turned to watch Cathy bundle the baby and hurry over to the resuscitation trolley, with the anaesthetist in tow. There was what seemed like minutes of silence, but was really only seconds, before a weak cry could be heard above the sound of the oxygen.

'Breathe, Noni.' Iain's voice penetrated the slight fogginess of her brain and she sucked in a sudden breath before letting it out.

'Thank you.' She blinked and concentrated on a few slow breaths and loosening her shoulders after the terrible tension. Her brain cleared and she looked down at the wound Iain was methodically tidying, having removed the placenta.

'How does the baby look?' Iain called across to the anaesthetist.

'Remarkably well, and very alert. No signs of cerebral irritation as yet. They'll keep an eye on her over in OB but I'd reckon she got off scot-free.'

Noni and Iain looked at each other and both smiled in relief. Then Noni remembered.

'So. You're a surgeon!' Her voice was carefully expressionless. She glanced at the now lustily crying baby. 'And a highly skilled one, at that.'

'Let's finish here first, shall we?'

'By all means, *Doctor*.' She saw him wince out of the corner of her eye as she stressed his title. A sudden chill ran down her spine as she realised where they would have been if Iain hadn't been around. But that didn't excuse his underhandedness—and his *lies*.

'I'll admit you did an incredible job to get that baby out so fast.' Her look promised more discussion at a different time.

He shrugged as if to say, I'll deal with it later. 'What time was the cord prolapse?'

Noni glanced at the theatre clock. 'Seventeen minutes ago.'

'Your very fast work getting her here will have made all the difference. Well done, yourself.'

'It must have been terrifying for Amanda.'

It took forty minutes to repair what had taken six minutes to open. But still the wound was of textbook neatness and Theatre Sister caught Noni's eye as she handed her back an instrument.

She whispered, 'He did it in half the time it normally takes. Impressive, eh?'

'I'll say,' Noni hissed back.

'OK, you two. Stop swelling my head.'

'But he's got really big ears.' Noni spoke in her normal voice and handed him the dressing to lay over the wound. Iain raised his eyebrows and Noni gazed blandly back.

He placed it gently over the wound and then stepped back. Noni watched him roll his powerful shoulders as if the great man had found some tension of his own.

'I'll see you later, then.'

Noni stared at him hard. 'Fine. I'll stay until Amanda wakes up and sees her baby.'

'Just forget I'm a doctor and treat me like a normal antenatal student.'

Noni raised her eyebrows. 'Even when you're obviously not normal?'

'Ha. Ha.' Iain tilted his head. 'Don't you have to get ready for classes?'

They had just finished dinner, and Iain got up to

take his plates into the kitchen. It was one of the little things that Noni liked about him.

Jacinta didn't even smile as she placed her plate on top of her father's. She'd been very quiet since she'd also found out Iain was a doctor.

Noni was over her shock now. 'So why did you choose surgery?'

'I really don't want to talk about it, OK?' Iain stalked off to the library.

Noni frowned. What was his problem? What was wrong with her being interested? She hoped later she'd be able to talk about some of her work concerns now she knew he'd understand. But it still didn't look too promising.

On Friday night, Noni stood at the doors of Maternity and watched the first of the cars pull up with the class members. The staff on duty had been discussing the threat of closure.

When everyone had assembled, she took the group on a tour of the ward, trying not to sound depressed when she pointed out the lovely, home-like surroundings.

They all sat down outside in the gazebo and she passed around the birthing suite goody-bag—a knapsack filled with items that could be used in labour. Everyone was to pull something out and try to explain what it was used for.

One young father-to-be pulled out a pair of men's swimming briefs and the class roared with laughter. 'I don't know what these are for!'

Noni forced her face to straightness and explained.

'Now, Paul, you may have to rub Suzie's back in labour while she's in the shower, and you're going to get wet if you do the job properly.'

'I wouldn't wear these.' He screwed his face up.

'That's fine,' Noni said kindly. 'We're all nurses in there with you so if you don't want to wear anything, it's OK.'

The class roared again. Iain's eyebrows had nearly disappeared into his hairline. Noni smiled serenely back at him. It was his turn to dip in to the bag. He pulled out a plastic toy camera.

'To take photos of the baby.' He took one look at Jacinta's face and added hastily, 'Not during the birth, of course.'

'Not likely.' Jacinta was pretending to scowl and the class laughed again.

Once the bag was empty, Noni ushered them into the birthing suite she'd prepared. The lights were dim, the aroma of lavender lingered faintly and rainforest music played softly in the corner. She had filled the bath up with mounds of soft bubbles and set out the mat and beanbag on the floor.

'Everything in here you could bring yourself if you had to. If you set your room up like this you can help yourself to stay as relaxed as possible while listening to what your body wants you to do. Remember what I've said. The contractions are good pains—the harder they are, the better they are doing their job. Don't fight them, work with them.'

She looked around at the interested faces, eager to understand how their bodies worked and what they could do to help. Even Iain was nodding his head.

'Stay relaxed so these good pains can push Baby's head against the cervix and help it open. Then sigh after the pain to get rid of any extra tension.' She looked at the nearest male. 'That's your job. Make sure she has let go of the last contraction and is resting before the next one.'

Before they finished for the night, Noni took them in to see a birthing unit which hadn't been prepared. 'If you were travelling somewhere and you had to have your baby in another hospital, it might look like this.'

The room was sterile, with steel furniture exposed, white sheets and bright lights. There was no music and it smelt like a hospital. 'I want you to envisage turning this room into the room next door.' Most of the class were nodding their heads, seeing her point. Then she saw Jacinta's face.

It had that look on it again. Noni could see her starting to shake and she tried to catch Iain's eye, but he was laughing with one of the fathers.

'Well, that's all, folks.' She pointed to the door. 'I'll see you next week back at our usual room.' She moved swiftly to Jacinta's side and steered her out of the room into the one next door.

'Jacinta! What is it?' She crouched down in front of the girl. Noni glanced up as Iain appeared at her shoulder. 'She's upset again.'

'Probably the stark reality of next door. Was that really necessary?'

'Fine. Let's pretend they don't usually look like that in the city.' Noni couldn't believe he could blame her for Jacinta's state. She ignored him then.

'What is it, honey?' She chafed the girl's hands.

'Tell him to go away.' The whispered words carried to her father. He stepped back as if he'd been slapped. Noni wished she could have softened the statement but he wasn't her first priority.

'Can you give us a couple of minutes, please, Iain?' He walked to the door, turned in a circle, opened his mouth but didn't say anything and finally walked away.

'Tell me the real reason you're in this state, Jacinta. I want to help you.'

The young girl looked up at her and Noni caught her breath. What she saw scared her. The brown eyes so like Iain's were filled with such pain she could hardly bear it. Maybe she should call Iain back? But Jacinta started to talk.

'My mum died having a baby,' she sobbed. 'The nurses wouldn't let me in, the room looked like that one—I saw it when they opened the door to come and go, and I could hear her scream. I couldn't save her.'

'Who was with you there, sweetheart?' Noni lifted the girl's cold little hand and wrapped her own warm ones around it.

'Her boyfriend.' The tears ran down her cheeks. 'That's why I moved into the flat with Reg. I couldn't go home and live with her boyfriend after she died.' She raised tortured eyes to Noni. 'If I'd rung my father he could have come and maybe he could have helped.'

Noni sighed with pain for the child in front of her. A child in a woman's body, carrying another child.

She could feel the sting of tears at the back of her own eyes and blinked them back.

'Sometimes people die having babies, Jacinta. It's a tragic part of nature. But usually it's because of another medical reason as well as pregnancy. Strong, healthy girls without medical illnesses don't die. *You* are not going to die having your baby.' Please, God.

'Your father will be there and he will make sure everything is right for you. Come on. Let your dad take you home. He's worried sick about you. And I'll be home soon, too.'

CHAPTER FIVE

NONI walked into the library. Iain was leaning with both hands on the mantelpiece. He looked up and shook his head.

'She told me. This bloody fiasco gets worse and worse. Jacinta didn't tell me in case I thought she wasn't really my daughter. Because her mother had a boyfriend.' He took a turn around the room. 'How I wish she'd been able to ring me.'

His eyes were deep pits of despair in the stone of his face. Noni didn't know how to comfort him.

'I can't get over Adele having the key to seventeen years of my child's life. Information that could have changed Jacinta's life.' His eyes were cold steel and his voice matched.

'How could a woman not tell a man he had a child?'

Noni winced. Easily. Harley's father didn't know about his son. This was definitely not the time to mention it. At some stage she would broach that subject, but for the moment Jacinta was the concern. They needed a plan.

'We need to find a way to reassure Jacinta. Dwelling in the past isn't going to help. She still thinks she's going to die in labour, like her mother did.'

His head shot up. 'That's it. I'll find out which

hospital it was and how Adele died. There had to be an underlying medical problem or someone stuffed up severely in Obstetrics. I'll find out and then she'll see it's not going to happen to her.'

He paced the room as if he wanted to leave now. 'I'll have to wait until Monday. The sort of search I'll need will have to go through a medical records department.'

Noni had a sinking feeling it wouldn't be easy to gain access to medical records in a strange hospital. He looked very determined, though, and she shrugged. It was hard to imagine Iain not getting his own way.

If he tried hard enough he'd probably get his own way with her. She blinked and felt a shiver cross her skin. Why would she think that? Because, she admitted the truth to herself, he'd started to intrude on her thoughts at odd moments. She noticed when he was there and she noticed when he was gone. Unfortunately, she was starting to feel more than a little alive when he was there.

Iain looked down at Noni. 'Will you and Win look after her for me while I go away?'

'Of course.' Her answer was almost a whisper while she wrestled with her own crisis. She was dangerously close to loving him. She cleared her throat and her voice strengthened. 'You don't have to ask that.' She had to get out of here. 'I'm going up to bed. Try and get some sleep.'

There was no way she would sleep tonight. Noni couldn't believe she had been so stupid. She'd made sure Harley knew Iain and Jacinta would leave a couple of days after the baby was born. How could she be falling for someone who was here for such a short while?

She sighed. The last man she'd been involved with had only been passing through, too.

Jacinta was very quiet over the weekend and Noni didn't feel much more talkative. By Sunday evening the house was positively morose.

Noni was worried about Jacinta and the added burden of the maternity ward's possible shut-down. It was less than four weeks until Easter, and if she lost her job there would be a major lifestyle change for them all.

She'd have to travel to the base hospital and wouldn't get the day shifts through the week she had now, plus weekends off. Aunt Win would lose her time away, Noni would see less of Harley and the money she budgeted would be hit severely with the cost of travel.

Then there was Iain. OK, she realised she could be in love, but she'd never been in love before. How did she know if it was the real thing or just proximity tricking her?

Iain was obsessed with his quest, and Noni was wary of asking too much in case he started on again about Jacinta's mother not informing him of her birth.

The only happy person was Harley. His cricket team had won. He was practising every day with Iain. His bubble burst when he found out Iain was going away for a week.

Noni was peeling potatoes at the table when she told him.

'Can I go with Iain, Mummy?'

She blinked. 'Don't be silly.'

Her son looked at her as if she had just crawled out from under a rock.

'That wasn't very dip-lo-mat-ic, Mummy.'

Noni dropped the peeler and sat back. Elephants never forgot. She played back what she'd said in her mind. Oops. 'You're right. I'm sorry, Harley. No, you can't. He's seeing lots of people and won't be able to spend time with you.'

'Can I ask him?'

Noni would have loved to have seen Iain's face when he did. 'If you want to. But it's not going to do any good.'

They were sitting around the table at teatime when it happened.

'Iain?' Harley had his I'm-an-angel look on.

Iain looked up from his plate. 'Yes, mate?'

'Can I come to Sydney with you, please?' Iain didn't say anything and he rushed on, 'I've never been to Sydney. I wouldn't be a nuisance and I know you have to talk to lots of people. I could sit in the car and make sure it didn't get stolen. Mummy said once that lots of cars get stolen in Sydney.'

Iain met Noni's eyes across the table. She looked blandly back. Never for a moment did she think he might say yes.

'If you mind my car and it's OK with your mummy, you can come.'

She knew he saw her mouth drop open. Her stomach dropped right through her body to the floor and she felt sick. The rat. Taking her baby away. He'd never spent a night away from her. She had been going to take him to Sydney some time soon.

Harley was whooping, Iain had continued with his tea as if it was no big deal and Jacinta was an interested bystander. Noni was horrified.

'I can go, can't I, Mummy? You said I could ask him.'

'What about school?' She searched her mind for reasons. 'Cricket practice? The dog?'

'We don't have a dog.' Harley smiled in relief. 'You're kidding me. Thanks, Mummy. Thanks, Iain. I'll call you Mr McCloud while we're away, I promise.' He jumped up from the table. 'I can pack my bag.' He rushed around the table and gave Iain a hug and then his mother one.

For a moment there Noni thought he was going to give Jacinta one, too. He took off and she heard him leaping up the stairs to his room. She sighed and caught Iain's eye on her. She pushed her plate away and got up.

'I'm going for a walk.' She heard the scrape of his chair.

'I'll come, too.'

Jacinta scowled. 'I suppose I have to wash up. I thought I was the guest.'

Noni turned her head. 'Leave it. I'll do it when I come back.'

'I would appreciate if you could do it, Jacinta.' Her father's voice was expressionless but his daughter hauled herself out of the chair anyway.

Noni breathed deeply when she hit the night air on the verandah. She could just smell the tang of salt, which meant the sea breeze was blowing their way. She felt Iain come up behind her and take her elbow. She shook his arm off.

'Let's go down towards the river mouth.'

At first he set off too fast and Noni found herself skipping every second step to keep up. She stopped. 'Hey. This is my walk. Slow down or go on your own.'

He looked down at her shorter legs next to his. 'Just a simple "Could you slow down, please, Iain?" would have been sufficient.'

She narrowed her eyes. 'In your dreams.'

He stopped and she went a few paces before she realised he was behind her. She stopped, too.

His voice came out of the dimness. 'Did you want to have a fight, or just bicker a bit for the fun of it?'

'Whatever you want, buster.' She stood there belligerently. Small and fierce. Her feet planted firmly on the ground and her fists clenched.

He came up to her and admired her stance. 'Actually, I didn't mean fisticuffs. But I know what I want.'

He pulled her into his arms and she stood there as stiff as a board, refusing to soften. She heard his breath whistle as he half laughed in the darkness. He bent down to look into her face.

'So. Resistance.' He kissed her brow and her cheek and the spot under her lips and the side of her mouth. Light kisses, tiny flutters against her skin that made her want to catch his mouth with hers. Then her ear and her neck and, finally, as light as a feather on her lips. But she didn't allow herself to respond even though every part of her wanted to. He stepped back.

'Hmm.' He took her hand and pulled her gently along until she fell into step with his slower walk. 'How about I tell you a story?'

She didn't say anything and he took it as encouragement.

'Once upon a time, there was a ferocious, white-haired mother ferret—'

'Ferret. Great, I'm a short, stumpy, white-haired ferret.'

'You're so vain! What makes you think I'm talking about you?'

She reached up and flicked him in the arm.

'I think ferrets are cute. Where was I? Oh, yes, a ferocious mother ferret. There was no father ferret and she was very protective of her baby ferret. By the way, she named him after a motorbike.'

Noni saw his teeth flash again and she had to smile. 'Get on with the story.'

'One day one of the senior handsome ferrets, who quite fancied this mother ferret, offered to take the baby ferret for a field trip. The mother ferret said yes but was very frightened in case something happened to her baby while she wasn't there to watch over him.' He looked down at her. 'Are you following this?'

'Don't push your luck!'

'But the mother ferret should have known that the senior handsome ferret would take care of the baby ferret as if he were his own. In fact, he left his own baby ferret with her to keep safe while he was away.'

'Is there a moral to this story?'

'How about, "You mind my ferret and I'll mind yours"?'

She laughed but it was half a sob.

Iain stopped and turned her to him. This time she leaned against him. 'It's OK, sweetheart. He'll be fine.'

'Yes. I know. It'll do him good to get away from his mother for once.'

He hugged her and kissed the top of her head. 'You are a wonderful, stupendous, fabulous mother, and he is a very lucky little boy.'

'You won't really leave him in your car, will you?'

He threw back his head and laughed. 'I promise I won't. If I have to leave him anywhere, my house-keeper can come in and mind him in the flat. OK?'

She did feel better. They turned around and started walking home hand in hand. When they arrived out-side the gate he stopped and pulled her gently into her arms. 'We'll be back on Friday before you get home from classes.'

He bent his head and she stretched up as high as she could until their lips met. 'Mmm. I've never kissed a ferret before.'

She flicked him again and he chased her into the house.

They left before she went to work the next morning. Harley was sitting up happily in the front seat of the Mercedes with a grin as wide as a banana. Still, Noni wiped tears away as the rear of the car disappeared down the street. Aunt Win put her arm around her but she, too, was in shock that Noni had let him go.

The week seemed to drag and they had a crisis meeting at work about the doctor shortage. Babies continued to arrive at all hours of the night and day and the staff were run off their feet.

Noni missed her little boy like an amputated limb. Then she found herself glancing at the clock all through the day as she wondered what Iain was doing. Harley phoned every night to talk to her and Jacinta answered her father's questions in monosyllables.

But Iain never asked to speak to Noni.

She was starting to wonder if it was his way of letting her know he wasn't interested in a relationship.

On Wednesday, Noni met Penelope in the post office.

'I hear Iain took your son to Sydney.' She shook her head as if she couldn't believe it.

'Yep. Nothing's a secret in this town.'

'Iain told me, of course. I was speaking to him last night. It seems a bit strange to take a child he hardly knows on such a big trip.' She smiled sweetly at Noni. 'But Iain always has been too kind for his own good.'

Noni smiled just as sweetly back. 'Yes. I heard he'd taken you out a couple of times as well. Such a nice man. See you.'

Noni fumed all the way home. She's a witch! But it was Iain she was angry with. How dared he talk to that woman and not to her?

She slammed the door behind her as she came in and stormed into the library, not sure why she was in there except it was the place she usually found Iain when he was at home. Jacinta looked up from the sewing machine her father had repaired.

'Noni? Can I talk to you?'

Her attention caught by Jacinta's tone, she stuffed her anger back in its place just behind her heart, then pulled a chair over to the little table beside Jacinta. 'Sure. What's up?'

'Iain said you had Harley when you were about my age. Were you scared about the labour?'

'I was nearly twenty when I had Harley. But, yes, I was terrified. You ask Aunt Win.' She smiled at the memory.

'Where was your mum?'

Noni sighed and pursed her lips as she ordered her thoughts. It was a time she didn't really like to think about. She settled herself comfortably as she thought about how to begin.

'I was born to my parents late in life. They adored each other and I sometimes wondered if I cramped their style a bit when I was born. My mother always said to wait until I found someone who made me feel like a queen before I made love.'

She smiled sadly. 'When I turned seventeen and left home, they did, too. They sold the house and joined a motorbike club for people over fifty. I thought they were mad but a lot of relatives on my Dad's side are pretty different. They were so happy being sixty-year-old rebels.'

Jacinta's eyes nearly popped out of her head. 'That's cool.'

'Yes. I suppose it was. I lived in the nurses' home,

anyway, while I did my nurse's training, so it didn't make much difference to me. One day they were at a bike rally, celebrating Woodstock memories or something, and there was a big pile-up of motorbikes on the expressway. They were both killed.'

'How horrible.'

'Yes, it was. I was pretty angry with both of them. I was actually wild with anger.' She swallowed at the thought of telling the next bit. 'So I went out and lost my virginity to a blues singer passing through town who found me crying.'

She looked at Jacinta. 'It was really for the comfort. He told me before we made love I'd never see him again. In case I wanted to change my mind. I guess I thought I was getting back at my parents, which was pretty dumb. Then I found out I was pregnant. Horrible bad luck, I thought at the time.'

'Did you tell him you were pregnant?'

'His band was gone the next day. I never tried to find him. He had a mischievous smile, which is what I remember most. We had nothing in common except that one night and he was much older than I was. I put ''Father Unknown'' on Harley's birth certificate. That was the only negative thing about having Harley. Apart from that, I wouldn't change a thing.'

'Who looked after you when you got really big, like me now?'

'Aunt Win. As I said before, I was terrified. She was with me through labour, just like your Dad and I will be with you. It's natural to be apprehensive about what you go through, giving birth to a child. Just remember you're designed to do it.

'I did an important thing before I had Harley. I went to my parents' graves and forgave them. And I asked them to forgive me for hating them. I finally realised it had been their choice to live their lives as they wanted. Imagine if, because of me, they were old and unhappy because they never realised their dreams. That's worse than dying.'

Jacinta nodded, taking it all in.

'So after Harley was born I became a midwife. For me, there's no other job better than being there and helping a woman realise she can do this difficult but rewarding task nature has set her.'

She slipped her arm around Jacinta's shoulders and squeezed them gently. 'Just like you will when your time comes.'

Jacinta didn't say anything for a few moments. Then she smiled and leaned over and kissed Noni's cheek. 'Thanks for that. I think I might go to my room for a while.'

Noni watched her lever herself out of the chair and head for the stairs. She felt drained and rested her head on her arms. She wouldn't change a thing about her life but was still glad she wasn't seventeen again!

Week five of antenatal classes included the visit from the obstetrician, Dr Soams, and a discussion on intervention in labour. It seemed strange without Iain's presence in her class, and it didn't help that everyone kept asking where he was.

Dr Soams explained the reasons a doctor would consider it necessary to take a hand in the natural process, and while sometimes Noni disagreed she held her tongue. She kept a wary eye on Jacinta's face.

It was a fact of life that a woman's labour sometimes didn't have the outcome she hoped for. Noni realised that if people knew the reasons it sometimes helped them come to terms with disappointment in the method of their baby's birth.

After Dr Soams left, Noni answered any questions and reiterated her favourite saying. 'Knowledge is power. So be aware of your choices and what is really necessary. Remember that the birth of your child is unique to you, and all you're doing is trying to make it the best in your particular circumstances.'

When the class broke up to go home, Jacinta came up to Noni.

'Why didn't they do a Caesarean section on my mother?'

Noni put her arm around Jacinta and looked into her face. 'That's what your father has gone to find out.' She smiled at the thought of seeing Harley.

'They should be home by the time we get there. You can ask him.' She grinned at the young girl beside her. 'I've enjoyed my week with you. Now the men are back our peace will be gone.'

CHAPTER SIX

WHEN Noni drove the ute into the garage at her usual pace she barely missed the Mercedes. Both women looked at each other and giggled.

'One day you'll hit it.'

'Only if he parks it in the wrong place. Then it'll be his fault.' They smiled at each other and got out.

'I heard that!' Both women jumped and turned to Iain who was leaning against the carport wall.

'He's got sonic ears, you know.' Noni winked at Jacinta. She looked around but couldn't see her son. 'Where's Harley?'

Iain tucked a woman under each arm and walked them to the house. For once Jacinta didn't pull away. 'He was waiting in the library for you but he's fallen asleep. I left him there in case he woke up.'

They settled in the library and Noni managed to slide herself under Harley so that he was sprawled in her lap. It felt good to hold him and she kissed his downy face.

She looked up at Iain who was leaning on the cold fireplace. She tried really hard not to be sidetracked into just staring at him. He looked good enough to eat. *Stop that*, she admonished herself.

'Jacinta and I have had lots of talks and we both want to know what you found out. Especially why they didn't do a Caesarean on Adele.'

He crouched down in front of Jacinta's chair and spoke slowly and gently.

'There wasn't time. Your mother had a heart condition she didn't tell anyone about. She should never have become pregnant again. The strain of the delivery caused a heart attack and I talked with the doctor in charge of her case. I believe they did everything possible to save her. After her attack they tried to save the baby before it died, too. But it wasn't possible.' He sat on the edge of his daughter's chair. 'I know it was horrific for you to be there but I truly believe that's what happened. Dr Soams will run a few tests to reassure you, but I believe it won't happen to you.'

There was silence in the room as his words died away. Jacinta stared into the empty fireplace and Noni's eyes traced the lines of strain on Iain's face. It hadn't been easy for him.

Jacinta looked up at her father unflinchingly. 'Thank you for finding out. I think I'll go to bed now. Goodnight.' She didn't look at either of them as she left the room and silence settled again.

'Would you like me to carry Harley up to his room?'

Noni hugged her son and smiled at the little snoring noises he was starting to make. 'Yes, thanks, he's out for the count.'

Iain lifted him and she wriggled the blood back into her legs before standing up. Her baby boy was getting quite heavy. It made her catch her breath to see her own son lying in Iain's arms, and she had a brief flash of other times he and Harley had shared. It was going to be hard on both her and Harley when Iain and Jacinta went back to Sydney. Very hard.

Noni had to hurry to beat Iain to her son's bed and turn back the sheets. She then tucked them around Harley's shoulders when Iain had laid him down. She stood back then straightened his head on the pillow. He grunted and rolled himself into a ball anyway.

It was so good to have Harley home. She felt as if someone had stitched her limb back on. She reached over to kiss his cheek. 'Love you, baby.'

She heard Iain leave the room and she stayed where she was, brushing the hair from her son's forehead as she thought about the changes in their lives these last few weeks.

She thought about the changes to come. Jacinta's baby's arrival. Her work and whether she would still have a job. Iain and Jacinta leaving not long after that. Iain and the tension building between them as they spent more time together. She rubbed her forehead.

He was starting to occupy a huge part of her daily life just in the amount of times she thought about him. Little memories of the way he laughed. How she was starting to hoard anecdotes of incidents she knew would amuse him. The hard part was to try and keep things in perspective.

Especially when all she wanted to do was lose herself in Iain's arms.

She'd missed him, too. More than she would have believed possible a couple of weeks ago. But she had to be sure of both their feelings before she did something stupid like fall in love. If it wasn't too late.

She stood up. 'Sweet dreams, Harley.' She pulled

the door half-closed behind her so that she would hear him if he called out, and walked slowly back down the stairs to the library.

Iain was reading the newspaper in the chair but Noni's lips twitched when she noticed it was upside down. It was nice to know she wasn't the only one who didn't know what to do about their mounting attraction.

'So, can stockbrokers read columns upside down?'

He turned the paper round the right way. 'Ah. That's much better, thanks.' He folded the paper and tucked it into the side of the chair and stood up.

Iain couldn't believe how much he'd missed her. He shoved his hands into his pockets to stop himself reaching out for her as she stood there, with head tilted, looking at him. How could such a tiny package contain so many contrasts? She was totally unaware of what it did to him, just to look at her.

'Is there much chance of you coming over here?'

She shook her head and they stood there, staring at each other across the room.

'How about we meet, say, at the table?'

Noni pursed her lips and nodded, and they both moved forward until they were standing together, almost touching. The top of her head rested under his chin and her face was level with his second top button.

'You know, I've put some thought to this positional problem we have. Would you like to hear it?'

'Uh-huh.' She nodded her head but she was actually savouring the faint drifts of aftershave that teased her nose. She really wanted to open that button of his shirt and bury her nose in his chest.

'Better yet, I'll show you.' He took her hand and knelt down on the floor, pulling her down on her knees as well. 'I think it could get better,' he said. Still holding her hand, they lay down on the carpet with elbows resting on the floor and their noses almost touching.

'That's better. Would you like to hear about my trip to Sydney with your son?'

She wanted his arms around her. It was crazy and she felt like she was balancing on the edge of some dangerous cliff. Maybe he thought lying here on the floor was good because he wanted some distance from her?

Noni frowned. Well, she had to find out. 'I'm not really comfortable. Can we go up to my room and lie on my big bed and talk there?'

She watched him blink and try to keep his face expressionless, but she saw the flare of emotion in his eyes. Her own lips twitched.

Iain was up and pulling her up after him before she knew what was happening. 'Gee, that's a hard one. OK.'

He dragged her behind him at a very fast walk and Noni started to giggle. Up the stairs to the top, where they slowed to an exaggerated creep past Harley's door and into Noni's room. Iain stopped inside the door and looked around.

'I really didn't take much notice that first day you had sunstroke. I've been trying to remember what your room was like. Now I remember. It's like I've walked into an underwater cavern.'

There were no floral doonas or lacy cushions—just different shades of blue and green in the curtains, and the bedcover and all the furniture was painted dark blue.

'I've never seen anything like it, but it's very restful.'

'What were you doing, imagining my room?'

He grinned at her. 'Purely from an interior decorator's interest, of course.'

'I thought you were a surgeon, or was that a stockbroker?'

'Yes, we have to talk about that.'

Noni stared at him. There was more? 'Help me fix these pillows so we can sit up comfortably, then.'

She felt him watching her and thought again about how much she'd missed him. What would she feel like if he went back to Sydney in a few weeks and she never saw him again? She sat up with her back against the wall and patted the bed beside her. She tried to keep her voice normal.

'Tell me about your week. I'm dying to know how you got on with Harley.'

Iain climbed up next to her and nudged her forward so he could slip his arm behind her shoulders. She snuggled against his chest and looked into his face. 'This is much more comfortable.'

It wasn't really. It was hard to stay sane.

What had possessed her to suggest coming up here? As if she didn't know. Then a black cloud descended. He hadn't even spoken to her on the phone once while he'd been away. She needed to hold that thought.

He looked back at her and then leaned over to kiss her firmly on the lips. 'Ready?'

'Before you begin, I have a bone to pick with you.'

He sat back with a sigh. 'It must be my technique. I kiss you and your mind remembers some trivia. What is it?'

'You rang that woman and yet you didn't ask to speak to me once while you were away.' She sat back away from his chest and folded her arms.

She watched him bite his lip to stop smiling. She hated that.

'I didn't really ring to talk to Penelope. I rang to ask her father about Jacinta's antenatal visit. But, yes, I spoke to her and not to you.'

'Why not?'

'Do ferrets sulk?'

'Don't start that again!'

Iain laughed out loud then. He pulled her resisting body back onto his chest and kissed the top of her head. 'Because I missed you like crazy and I wanted to talk to you in person, not over a stupid phone. All right?'

He stared into her eyes and she knew it was the truth.

She'd pay for that. In fact, she would memorise it and store it for ever.

'OK. You can start telling me about Sydney now.' She slid off his chest to lie beside him. Then snuggled in as close as she could get. Unconsciously her hand lifted to play with the button she'd wanted to undo on his shirt.

Noni felt his chest rise as he drew a deep breath and then his hand came up and covered hers.

'If you keep doing that I'm not going to be talking at all. Maybe we should go back to being uncomfortable on the library floor.'

She smiled a woman's smile. 'I'll be good.'

'Why doesn't that make me feel better?' He sighed again just to tease her. 'Fine. We arrived on Monday afternoon and Harley thinks my flat is cool. Did I tell you I overlook Luna Park, beside the harbour?'

She shook her head. 'You haven't told me anything about your life in Sydney.'

Or your work. Or your family, if you have any. But she thought she'd better save those gripes for later. Then there was the point that Harley had seen his first amusement park without her. She wouldn't dwell on that either. She tuned in again and had to concentrate to catch up.

'That evening, I rang some people I know who have access to the particular hospital concerned, and they said they'd get back to me the next day.'

She was sceptical it had been that easy but she didn't say anything.

'Harley and I did the movies in George Street and we had tea up on Centerpoint Tower.' He smiled at the memory. 'He was pretty impressed with the night skyline from the tower and loved the lift ride up there.'

There was something in his voice that intrigued her. 'Didn't you like it?'

Iain shuddered. 'That building sways in the wind. Harley practically had his nose pressed to the glass, looking down. It made me feel sick and he was getting tired of me telling him to get back from the edge.'

'Poor baby. I think you're very brave, taking my son up there, if you don't like heights.' She reached over and kissed the little triangle of skin below the collar of his shirt.

'Yes. I was.' He turned to face her. 'How about I just kiss that bit of skin on you?'

'On with the story.'

He tut-tutted. 'Very unsportsmanlike. The next day I left him with my housekeeper until lunchtime but she's a whiz on the Internet so they had a great time.'

'Are we talking housekeeper or au pair?'

'She's a grandmother.'

'So? You'll be a grandfather and you're only thirty-nine.'

He wiggled his eyebrows suggestively a few times. Then became serious. 'Quiet, woman.'

Noni snuggled back and rested her cheek on his shoulder.

'I talked to some people and tracked down the doctor in charge of Adele's case. Apparently, she didn't come into the hospital until almost the last minute so it would have been pretty scary for Jacinta at home with her.'

She squeezed his arm in sympathy.

'On Wednesday, I found out the name of Adele's boyfriend and tracked him to Redfern. He wasn't as bad as I'd worried he'd be. He's still upset over Adele's and the baby's death.

'He seemed genuinely relieved I had Jacinta. He'd heard she was pregnant but said she hadn't spoken to him since her mother died. Said she blamed him, but he blamed himself anyway. I'm pretty sure he didn't know about Adele's heart condition or I think he would have taken her to hospital earlier. Hopefully he can get on with his life now that he knows a bit more.'

She squeezed his arm again. 'You did well, tracking everyone down. I also think Jacinta will be more settled now that she knows.'

'I hope so. I don't think her mother had much of a life, and I've a lot of making up to do.' He seemed to shake himself to get rid of the bad memories.

He went on. 'But to Harley. On Thursday we took the ferry to Taronga Park Zoo, which was a huge success, I might add, and caught the hydrofoil back. We visited the museum.' His eyes crinkled at the memory. 'And Harley's a mummy's boy.'

She knew he was waiting for her to bite. 'Ha, ha. I loved the mummies, too, when I went to the museum.'

He nodded his head, acknowledging her point. 'Friday morning, I dropped in at work and Harley sat in the car—just kidding—then we came home after lunch. I think he had a good time. He slept on the way home so I didn't get any conversation out of him.'

He slid his arm out from under her shoulders and clasped his hands behind his neck with an innocent expression on his face. 'So that's my story. What are we going to do now?'

'Why, talk about my week, of course.' She leaned across and kissed him on the lips.

His hands came from behind his neck faster than she could move away, and he captured her face and rolled her body onto him in one movement. She was resting on his chest, looking into his face, before she knew it. She could feel the hardness of his body against hers and she felt the fever he caused in her bubbling away below the surface. If she didn't move now she was going to spontaneously combust.

He seemed quite happy about it, though. 'Now, that's a comfortable position for us to talk,' he said.

She sat up, let her legs fall to either side of his body and tucked her knees up to sit upright on his chest, looking down. 'Ha! I'm looking down on you for a change.'

'I can cope with this.' He lifted his hips and she rose in the air. 'Ride me, cowgirl.'

Noni blushed. She felt his hardness through the clothes they wore and the heat glowed in her belly in response. She needed some space between them. Now. 'Ah, I'd better get down from here. I think my horse is smarter than I am.' She slid off his chest and tucked her feet up under her bottom. 'Do you want to hear about my week or not?'

His expression became more remote and she wasn't surprised when he said, 'Love to, but can we get something to eat first?'

He was slipping off his side of the bed as he spoke, and Noni narrowed her eyes as she watched him move towards the door. She didn't say anything. He'd deliberately cut her off. Why? There had to be a reason because she really didn't believe he was that shallow. But she couldn't help the disappointment that gnawed at her. She slid off the bed and followed him.

Noni never did get to tell him about her week. By the time she'd made a late supper and Aunt Win had reappeared, after 'giving them time to catch up', it never made its way into the conversation. She wondered if her side of the story ever would.

When she lay in bed that night she mulled over Iain's disinterest in her work at the hospital. Did he have a reason or was he just incredibly self-centred? Did she have room in her life for someone who might be fairly demanding and yet give only a small piece of himself back? Maybe she was better keeping the status quo. But what did she do about the fact that she was starting to feel only half alive when he wasn't around?

After Saturday cricket, they arrived home in separate cars as Noni had refused Iain's offer of transport.

She planned to try and avoid him as she grappled with her confused thoughts and feelings. She really didn't have any prior experience to draw on, and she hated not knowing what she was doing.

The few times that morning Iain had tried to engage her in conversation she'd been very unforthcoming. Now, as she came through the door he held open for her, she pulled her body noticeably out of the way of any possibility of brushing up against him.

Aunt Win looked at both of them and pulled her cardigan tighter across her shoulders. 'Brr,' she said.

Iain just frowned and disappeared into the hallway.

'Do you want me to stay home this weekend, honey?' They were in the kitchen and Win was about to leave. She tilted her head and searched her niece's face.

'No. We'll manage fine. You have your time out. If my work problems don't resolve themselves there might be too few of your weekends to come.'

The older woman hugged her. 'Don't worry, Noni. We'll manage, whatever happens.' She picked up her bag and keys. 'Don't let a man get you down. But don't be stubborn either.' With those cryptic comments she opened the door and sailed out.

'Yeah, right. That makes sense,' Noni grumbled at the closed door.

'What makes sense?' Iain was leaning on the door from the library.

'You and your ears are getting right up my nose this weekend. I'll be glad when you're gone.' She knew it was a terrible thing to say—plus, it wasn't true—but she couldn't do anything about it now. She pushed past him and ran up the stairs to her bedroom.

Iain followed her progress up the stairs with his eyes. She still had the sexiest backside he had ever seen. He grinned as he tried to visualise an ear going up a nose and couldn't. She made him laugh.

As for Noni being glad when he was gone, well, he didn't think that was true either. Obviously something had upset her and he was sure she would tell him what it was sooner or later. She ran her life like her antenatal classes. Up front and with a passion. Trouble was, it was becoming harder to keep his fantasies about that passion under control.

He just wasn't ready for commitment after his last marriage fiasco. Noni deserved better than that. Maybe she could move in with him. His practice made enough money to keep them both in a very comfortable lifestyle. He could end up with a family of five before he knew it. Two months ago that would have been a horrible thought—now it was looking almost appealing. He went into the kitchen and had a look to see what Win had put out for tea. He'd make it and Noni would calm down and maybe they could go back and 'talk' in her room again.

This time he would close the door. He started to whistle as he worked.

Noni was lying across her bed. This was so unlike her. She hated these see-saw emotions Iain caused in her. She hated not being in control. For the last five years, with Aunt Win's help, she'd known where she stood and where she was going.

She'd really enjoyed Iain's company for the first few weeks. She enjoyed their verbal sparring. But she had to admit she was starting to think serious thoughts about him. Worrying about his relationship with Jacinta and trying to heal the breach between father and daughter. She ached for his guilt at not helping Adele and worried about how he was going to cope with Jacinta in labour and after the baby was born.

His voice gave her shivers and she loved the little

gestures that amused her, like opening doors for her and worrying about her safety.

But was she being foolish to fall for a man she really didn't know? What about the risk she exposed Harley to if Iain moved out of their lives like he was supposed to in a few weeks. Harley was becoming very attached to Iain. She couldn't believe she hadn't been more careful of that.

Lately she'd felt Iain didn't take her seriously at all. He wasn't interested in her life, apart from what affected him. He never asked about her job, never talked about his. She didn't even know his dead wife's name or how long they'd been married. She wanted to know about his childhood and his life in Sydney. She needed him to want to know more about her.

Their relationship, if that was what it was, was all on the surface. She knew he found her attractive, but there was more to life than sex, which was lucky or she wouldn't have had a life at all except for that one time. She gave a half laugh, half sob. There was no doubt in Noni's mind—with Iain it would be pretty wonderful sex. Just the thought of him had her nerves humming in anticipation. But was that all it would be? Sex?

Then what?

Maybe she should have asked Aunt Win to stay home. She punched the pillow. She had to go back downstairs and make tea. And she hated being at odds with Iain.

CHAPTER SEVEN

'WHAT are you doing here?' Noni stood at the kitchen door with her hands on her hips.

Iain gave a mock bow. 'Making tea so that the mistress of the house will be happy tonight and grant me favours.'

She tilted her head. 'Well, that was honest.' She watched him breathe a sigh of relief and had to smile. She wandered over and leaned against him.

'I'm lost here. I don't know what to do or not do, Iain. Have we got a relationship or are we playing games? If it was only me, it would be no big deal. But Harley is involved and he's getting very fond of you.' She pretended to frown. 'But he just spent a week with you. And you were hard on him at cricket today. He may hate your guts at the moment.'

Iain wiped his hands on a towel and put his hands around her waist. 'Going up.' He lifted her up until she was sitting on the kitchen bench and their eyes were level.

'That is one of the many things that blow me away about you. Your honesty.' He ran his finger down her cheek and kissed her nose. 'I will endeavour to be as honest. To answer your questions…' He ticked them off on his fingers.

'One, we haven't got a relationship—yet! But it's quite possible in the very near future.

'Two, we are playing games and I thought you were enjoying them.

'Three, my poor marital history is the reason I'm not rushing into a commitment. I don't want to risk destroying anyone else's life.

'Four, Harley does not hate my guts and I realise he shouldn't become too attached to me in case we decide this thing between us isn't going to work out.' He kissed her nose again.

'Any more questions, Miss Please-Spell-It-Out?'

Noni pursed her lips. 'No. That just about covers it. You can go back to your cooking now.'

'Gee, thanks. What about my favours?'

Noni felt the hairs rise on her arms at the look in his eyes. She could feel her brain turn to mush as her hormones took over, and she moistened her lips with her tongue. She had trouble finding her voice. 'I'll consider the type of reward after we've eaten.' It was lame but at least she'd said something.

'Can I have a down payment?' He slid his hips in between her legs as they hung over the front of the bench and encouraged her to wrap her lower body around him while his hands cupped her buttocks. It felt as if she'd stepped into a hot bath that made her ache with heat. So this was what she hadn't realised she was missing!

'I want to kiss you, Noni.'

'I'm afraid I want to kiss you, too.' He stared into her eyes. She could see her own reflected right back at her. She sighed. 'But if I do I may not want to stop.'

'I can live with that,' he said.

When his lips came down on hers, she slid her arms around his neck and she didn't get a chance to think about anything else. He was there. Strong yet tender. Her own need for him took over as she kissed him back, his breath and hers in an endless, mindless melding of mouths. It felt so right, and hard to stop.

By the time they broke apart, Noni's breath was coming in quick gasps and she could feel the heat spiralling up her belly from where he pressed against her.

Great waves of longing, or need, or just plain old lust assailed her. She'd never lusted after a man before, or really ached to know the meaning of possession. Her body was trying to work out how to get him up to her room when he kissed her again.

She pressed against him, squirming to get closer, and she didn't hear herself moan with the force of her arousal.

Iain did. He softened the kiss and gently pulled away to look at her. He stepped back and brushed the hair of her fringe out of her eyes. Her face was flushed and her pert little breasts were rising and falling with the air she was dragging into her lungs.

'God, you are the sexiest woman I have ever seen or kissed. And as much as I'd like to take you here on this bench, I really don't think this is the place to go any further.'

Noni blushed. 'My God! What happened?' She looked around the room and it was the same kitchen she had been standing in before. But *she* was different. Blown away. Definitely not in control.

He lifted her down and hugged her swiftly. 'It's

OK, sweetheart.' He patted her bottom and shooed her towards the door. 'But I'd really appreciate it if you could take that delectable body out of my sight while I try to calm down my libido.'

She glanced down at the noticeable bulge in his trousers and blushed again. She didn't say anything, just turned and walked mindlessly out of the door. She bumped straight into Jacinta's shoulder, even though the girl tried to avoid a collision.

Noni blinked. 'I'm sorry. I didn't see you. Are you all right?'

Jacinta's brows drew together and she tilted her head. 'Are *you* all right? You look weird.'

Noni gave a half-hysterical laugh and shook her head. 'I'm going up to my room.' She wandered off up the stairs and the girl shook her head in bewilderment.

'Hello everyone. Welcome to week six. Only two more weeks to go until the end of classes.' Several of the women, who looked very close to their time, laughed nervously.

'Later tonight we're going to talk about breastfeeding, but first we'll discuss the social differences that affect you when you have a baby.'

Noni grinned evilly. 'I really love to target this at the people who say their children aren't going to change their lives.' She rubbed her hands together like a short blonde wicked witch.

Iain bit back a smile. He savoured these antenatal classes as much for the good he could see they were doing Jacinta as for the enjoyment he gained from watching Noni in action. She was totally unselfconscious, managed to get the point across, usually with humour, and was never boring. In fact, she was the least boring woman he'd ever known.

He chuckled at indelible memories of Noni contorting her own body as if she were deep in the throes of labour on her hands and knees. He was starting to realise how much he was counting on Noni for her support through Jacinta's labour. Which was pretty amazing, considering he'd attended hundreds of births as an obstetrician. But, then, he'd never attended one as a father before.

The birth was something he hadn't given much thought to other than that Jacinta would probably hate it. He had never really appreciated the magnitude of fear and expectation a pregnant woman put into her birth experience.

He laughed at himself. Noni had him calling it a 'birth experience' after six classes and he'd called it 'labour and delivery' for the last fifteen years. He wouldn't dare to say he 'delivered a baby' to Noni. He knew she'd say it was the woman who gave birth and he only caught them! Which reminded him. He'd better clarify his profession to Noni—and soon.

He'd avoided talking about her work so he wouldn't have to lie any more about his own. He hadn't wanted her to pressure him into staying here as Burra's new obstetrician—but that was just ridiculous. Noni couldn't pressure him into doing anything he didn't want to, and the longer he went, not telling her about his true profession, the more inexcusable it was.

'Are you with us, Iain?' Noni could see he was a million miles away and she had a feeling he really hadn't given much thought to the time after the baby was born. There were some major lifestyle changes coming up for him as well as Jacinta.

'This is the class where I enjoy watching the reactions of the parents-to-be. I break you up into two groups and ask each group to write down all the changes you can think of that might happen after your baby is born.'

She grinned at the women. 'The men especially start to realise how much of a difference one little baby can make. You mums have a fair idea already.'

After half an hour of suggestions the two group answer sheets were compared in case some changes were missed. One of the fathers said, 'Why didn't we think about this beforehand?' Everyone laughed.

Jacinta was scowling at her father and Noni wasn't quite sure why. But it didn't look good.

Finally Jacinta let her feelings out. 'It doesn't seem fair that some people don't suffer at all. If you didn't know about your baby it wouldn't change your life a bit.'

There was silence in the room and Noni was searching her brain for some way to postpone the thinly disguised bitterness, at least until they got home, but Iain spoke up.

He stood tall and faced his daughter. 'Jacinta, in front of all these people, I swear that I would give anything to have known about your birth and been there when you learned to walk and talk and twist people around your little girl's finger. I feel just as ripped off as you do, and as for what I would have had to have given up…'

He looked around the room at Noni, all the prospective parents and finally at his daughter.

'If I'd had to give up everything on every list we could make so I could have those years back—I would!'

Noni felt the tears prickle at the back of her eyes and the silence in the room seemed to last for ever, but in reality it was only a few seconds.

The father who had spoken up before clapped Iain on the back. 'I wouldn't change back to not wanting children either.' He smiled at his young wife, and all the love he had for her was there in his face. 'We can't wait.'

Everyone started to talk at once and Noni sagged with relief. She bit her lip as she watched Jacinta stand up and move to her father's side, and for the first time she gave him a hug. Noni stayed back. They needed to share this moment between the two of them.

God was performing miracles again. She swallowed the lump in her throat. 'Let's go for supper now.'

'This hour we're going to talk about breastfeeding. You have all heard the slogan, ''Breast is Best''.' She looked around at the nodding heads.

'Breastfeeding is cheap, designed especially for your baby and is always on tap at the right temperature.' She held up her doll. 'This isn't the most effective way to learn, but I'll run through a few pointers. Hopefully it will cut down on early problems with the first few feeds in hospital.'

Iain was intrigued to see how Noni was going to handle this. She'd asked everyone to bring in a large doll or stuffed animal, to get the feel of holding the baby. He couldn't see how that was going to help.

'Right, I would like you all to imagine you are holding your baby.' There were lots of chuckles and comments about ugly babies.

'Then slide one hand back to support baby's head and the other arm tucks the body in close to you. Your baby should be almost wrapped around you chest to chest.'

Iain watched her go around the circle of people, checking and realigning any positions until she was satisfied.

He waited for her to come to him but she didn't. She was a wimp. He was being ripped off here. He put up his hand.

'My baby won't suck.' His eyes dared her.

His daughter looked at him as if he were mad and the other men in the class were grinning.

He knew Noni wouldn't shirk the challenge. Although he wasn't sure if it had been a good idea, judging by the wicked look in her eye.

'Come here, mother.' She flipped open the top two buttons of his shirt and slid her hand inside against his chest. 'You have to let Baby get at you. Don't be shy. How's that?'

Iain tried to stop his ears going red and the class was egging her on. The feel of her warm hand brushing his nipple made him catch his breath, but luckily she took it away before he made a complete fool of himself. He looked up at her face so close to him and felt better when he saw she was blushing, too. Serves us both right, he thought, and winked at her.

She moved hurriedly along and avoided his eyes. He tried to think cooling thoughts. He *really* enjoyed these classes! He stopped listening and concentrated on watching, as Noni slowed and became absorbed in what she was saying.

Her hand was pointing to her breast, circling it as she explained something, and even pushed the fabric of her shirt right in to demonstrate what an inverted nipple was.

He felt his chest tighten as she cupped her breast in one hand, rounding it up as if offering it to a baby. Iain shifted in his seat. His trousers must have shrunk in the last wash.

Her nipples were more noticeable through her shirt when she dropped her hand and he fantasised about the feel of them between his fingers.

'Dad?' Jacinta was looking at him strangely.

'Sorry, did you say something?' He played back the last couple of seconds of noises from the room. It was the third time she had called him. Then he realised something else.

'You called me Dad!' He grinned at her. 'It sounded good, too.' He leaned over and squeezed her hand. 'Did you want me for something?'

'I said could you get me one of those microwave sterilisers for the bottles? I'm not going to breastfeed.'

He blinked and bit back his first response, which

was to say, Of course you are. It was hard but he had a feeling he was being tested here.

'How about we talk about it when we get back to Noni's?'

He watched Jacinta raise her eyebrows but thankfully she said nothing further.

This really rocked him. He suddenly realised that at the end of the pregnancy there really would be a baby. A helpless being that had to have decisions made for it. Had to be looked after. A baby that needed the best care and nutrition. That meant breastfeeding—but Jacinta said she wasn't going to breastfeed.

He supposed she didn't have to feed the baby herself but he'd assumed she'd want to. As an obstetrician he encouraged breastfeeding for health reasons, but he'd never really felt strongly about it. Yet this time he did. He'd get Noni to talk to her.

His grandchild should really get the best.

He waited until they arrived home in his car.

They travelled together now. He'd finally been able to get through to Noni. He didn't like her left on her own to lock up. 'Can you go ahead, Jacinta? I want to ask Noni something.'

His daughter gave him an old-fashioned look. 'Yeah, right. Does she need another hug?' But she still went.

They sat in the car together and he was thinking about giving Noni another hug, instead of telling her why he'd wanted to speak to her privately.

'Yes? What did you want to ask me?' Noni was peering at him in the darkness.

His urge intensified with her voice. It was dark in
the car and he could barely make her out. It really
made him listen to the way she spoke. Husky and
incredibly sexy. He wanted to hear her making soft,
husky noises while he made love to her—and this was
one of the reasons he hadn't talked to her on the
phone from Sydney. It drove him crazy!

He leaned towards her and captured her hand.
'Hmm?'

'Hello, Iain? Is anybody home except hormones, or
was Jacinta right and you want to give me a hug?'

He sat back. Right. Breastfeeding. 'Jacinta wants
to bottle-feed.'

It was Noni's turn to sit back. So he didn't want
to give her a hug. Fine. She frowned and thought
about his statement. 'So she doesn't breastfeed.
What's the problem?'

He couldn't believe it. 'This is *my* grandchild
here—he should be breastfed. "Breast is Best" and
all that. You're a midwife. How can you say any dif-
ferently?'

'As a midwife, of course I advocate breastfeeding.
As a mother, I breastfed Harley, but as a friend of
Jacinta's I support her decision. She's the one that
has to do it.' She peered at him again, trying to see
the expression on his face.

'I don't believe this! Breast milk helps babies' im-
mune systems, has essential components to encourage
brain development and prevents sensitivity to aller-
gies. Why wouldn't I want that for my grandchild? I
want you to talk her into breastfeeding.'

She could hear the anger in his voice and it unsettled her. This was a side of him she hadn't seen.

'Excuse me? This child may be your grandchild but it's *Jacinta*'s baby. I'll listen to her reasons for choosing not to breastfeed and, as I've said, I'll support her in her decision. You're losing the plot here. I'm not going to talk her into anything she doesn't want to do.'

'*I'm* losing the plot?' His voice vibrated with suppressed anger. 'I ask you to do a simple little thing for me and you won't.' He opened the car door and climbed out. '*I'll* tell her.'

Noni sat in the car on her own and sighed. He would blow it! Jacinta had just started to call him Dad, too. She should get out and try to stop him. Explain her reasons and try to get him to see Jacinta's point of view.

She didn't. His anger was an eye-opener. She wouldn't have believed he was so narrow-minded and authoritarian. It was better to find out now but it made her sad. Like she'd just found out her idol had feet of clay. Oh, she knew he wasn't perfect, but she hated the thought that he really was so much the dictator. A relationship with him wouldn't work because she liked her own way, too. She almost smiled at another thought. Jacinta had enough of her father in her to fight her own battles.

She got out of the car and went in the back door through the kitchen to Aunt Win.

Her aunt's face lit up as she came in the door and her arms opened. 'Hello, Noni, love.' After their embrace, she stepped back to look at her niece's face and pursed her lips. 'How was your class?'

'Class was fine. It's Iain who's being a pain.' She lifted the lid of the biscuit barrel and snaffled a still warm Anzac biscuit. Noni chewed, swallowed, then went on.

'Jacinta wants to bottle-feed and Iain doesn't think that's good enough for *his* grandchild.' Aunt Win didn't say anything so she reached for another biscuit.

'So why doesn't Jacinta want to breastfeed?'

Noni shook her head. 'I don't know. I haven't had a chance to ask her. Iain doesn't seem to think she has a choice and I'm worried about the way he's starting to think. The baby is Jacinta's, not his. You never did that to me.'

Win snorted. 'As if it would have done me any good.'

Noni thought for a moment. 'No. If you didn't agree with something I had chosen to do, you respected the fact that it was my choice. I have never felt threatened that you wouldn't love me if I didn't do what you wanted or thought best.'

She looked at her aunt. 'You're pretty wonderful, you know. I hope I can remember all this when things get sticky between Harley and me.' She stretched up and kissed her aunt on the cheek. 'I think I'll give the others the slip and go to bed. Will you send Harley up before you go to bed, so I can talk to him, please?'

'Sure, love.'

Noni showered, changed into her satin pyjamas and lay on her bed, staring up at the ceiling in the semi-darkness. She could just see the luminous stars she'd

stuck there in the form of southern hemisphere con-
stellations. It had taken her hours, neck bent on the
ladder, to stick them up. Aunt Win had stood underneath, astronomy book in her hand, directing the positions.

Whenever she had really weighty matters to think
over, she found that staring up at them calmed her
mind. So why wasn't she calm?

Iain was really getting to her. When he arrived
she'd known he was trouble. Why hadn't she been
more careful? She should have known he would turn
out to be a huge complication in her life.

Yet at times he seemed to be her soul mate, their
minds running parallel and senses of humour matching perfectly. And last weekend's passion in the
kitchen had blown her away.

The arousal she'd experienced tonight in the middle of her antenatal class had shocked her, too. She'd
touched men's chests before and felt their hearts beat
under her hand. She certainly hadn't wanted to rip
their shirts off and run her hands all over them like
she'd wanted to tonight.

She was going under here. But she'd felt very let
down with Iain's attitude to Jacinta's decision to bottle-feed her baby.

She imagined some women would have seen nothing wrong with his assumptions, but she'd been there.
She'd been the teenage mum in the position where
everyone assumed they knew more than she did.
Thank goodness she'd had Aunt Win right beside her,
saying, 'You know best, he's your child.'

No matter how hard she strained her brain, she couldn't imagine Iain saying that to Jacinta.

No. A relationship with Iain McCloud wouldn't work—he would try to control them all. She couldn't let him. She was strong enough to withstand him.

As long as he didn't touch her or she didn't touch him.

That was the problem. Every day she woke up and wondered if this was the day she was going to make love with Iain. She was mad. Mad with lust!

He really was shallow, though. He never asked how her day had been when she came home from work. Wasn't really interested in her at all except for her body. Unfortunately her body was interested in his, too. It was all too confusing.

Then Iain's head came around the door and his body followed it.

'Win said you were up here.' He spoke very quietly as he peered into the darkness towards the bed.

'Did she tell you I didn't want to see you tonight?' Her voice trembled a little as her traitorous senses refused to hate him. She did *not* want to see him. She rolled over and turned her back to him. 'I'm tired. Goodnight.'

She listened for the sound of him leaving. He moved so quietly that she couldn't tell if he'd gone or not. It was killing her not to roll back and look. The door clicked shut and she sighed.

CHAPTER EIGHT

IAIN'S voice came out of the darkness beside her. 'Did you move to make room for me? Thanks.' Then she felt the bed shift as he climbed on and lay down beside her.

'Get out, Iain. I'm not in the mood for games tonight.'

'I'm not here for the fun of it, Noni. I hate apologising and haven't had much practice.' He put his hand on her shoulder and rolled her back to face him.

'You were right. It is Jacinta's prerogative to decide how to care for her child.' He chuckled in the dark. 'She blasted me out of the water when I said she had to breastfeed. Said I could do it if I was so in favour of it. You would have loved it.'

Noni relaxed slightly. 'So why doesn't she want to breastfeed?'

'She said she's not flipping her breasts out for everyone to see—she hates the thought and she just doesn't want to.'

'That's a valid reason and common with young, self-conscious girls. Some women don't like it. I can't think of much worse than a baby at his mother's breast, getting the message that she doesn't like him being there. It has to be much better to bottle-feed and enjoy holding and feeding your baby.'

'I see that now.' His voice became more rueful.

120

'Can we go back to the part in the car where I wanted to hug you?'

Noni could feel herself softening towards him. That was what happened. Just when she conceded that to get closer to him was a bad move, here she was, next to him on her bed in the dark. With the door shut.

'Harley is coming up to say goodnight to me in a minute.' She didn't say, Thank goodness, but it was in her voice.

'Win said to tell you she tucked him in.' His voice held the smugness that infuriated her.

She reached back and smacked him in the head with a pillow. Thwack. 'Well, ask her to tuck you in, too.' She moved to sit up and he rolled over, pulled her back and pinned her down with his body.

'Ferocious little ferret, aren't you?' His breath tickled her face and his arms pinned hers by her side. 'Let me apologise and then I will leave you alone.'

She stared at a star over his left shoulder and didn't say anything.

'Has to be that good, eh?' He let go of her arms and stroked a strand of fringe out of her eye. He rubbed his chest lightly against hers and rolled off.

'I'm sorry. You were right. I was a pig.'

He stood up and she missed him already.

'Arrogant pig!' she stated.

'Arrogant pig. Can I lie down again now?'

Her eyes were accustomed to the dark now and she could see him smile. Her body said, Yes. Please. And the rest of her agreed.

He slid down next to her and she snuggled into his

side to lie facing him. She played with the button on his shirt.

He stroked her cheek. 'You know, I thought my trousers had shrunk tonight when you were demonstrating the way to latch a baby onto your nipple.'

She smiled. 'Can I just undo these two buttons again?' Her hand reached in as she had in the class and he groaned.

His skin felt firm and warm and Noni's fingers slid across the solid bulge of his chest until she found one of his small nipples. To her delight, it hardened instantly in response to her touch. She looked up and the heat in his eyes woke the wanton in her. She felt powerful, desirable and strangely assertive. Her own body quickened and she came back to his other buttons to undo them all until she could push back the shirt. His chest lay very broad and bare, but for the few dark hairs in the shallow valley that drew her hands.

'Where does this road go?' She mused as she traced the darker line down his midriff.

Iain chuckled. 'I think straight to trouble, woman. Now give me your hands.' He caught her mischievous hands in one of his and held them, then dropped a swift, sweet kiss on her lips.

'Does your door have a lock?'

'I suppose it does, but I've never used it.' She watched him slide across the bed and pad to the door. Her heart was thumping and she could feel the heat in her cheeks. Thank goodness it was fairly dark. He'd think she was an idiot for starting this then being nervous.

The lock clicked and he came back and discarded his flapping shirt on the bedside table, before climbing back onto the bed. Then he was beside her and his arms were around her and it didn't matter about her nerves any more. His hands ran up her body and he proved he was much quicker at removing clothes than she was. Before she knew it there was only her skin against his and together they felt like silk on silk.

His lips met hers and it was as if they had both been shipwrecked for days without water. The kiss seemed to go on for ever and Noni felt as if she'd fallen into an ocean of sensations. All she could do was hold onto the lifeboat that was Iain and exult in the storm.

Once he whispered, 'There are a hundred places I've wanted to kiss for weeks.' And broke away to kiss the hollow of her throat, the skin beneath her ears and the valley between her breasts. Each place seemed to glow after his lips had been there, and she didn't know how much more of this she would be able to stand. She heard his murmured endearments, and even some tiny moans of her own, and then she pulled his lips back to hers and was lost again. She ran her hands over him and his skin was smooth under her fingers and she couldn't believe she was here with him finally.

An aching need grew in her belly and she rubbed herself against him more urgently.

In the eye of the storm he stopped, and removed something from his shirt pocket.

Noni lay back and in a brief moment of sanity she

smiled. There were times when having a control freak in charge did help.

Then he pulled her to him and she forgot the mundane matters of safety and discovered the ethereal world of losing herself in a man. The power and wonder in both of them met and exploded into something dazzlingly magical.

Afterwards, he cradled her against him and she could hear the pounding of his heart, matching her own. They dozed for a while under the quilt Iain had pulled over them both.

She turned her face and kissed the side of his chest. She loved him.

He was awake, too, and smiled down at her.

'I'm not sure how this will change our relationship, but I can't regret making love with you. It was beautiful,' she told him candidly.

He kissed the top of her head. 'You were beautiful and I love your honesty.'

'Well, if we're being honest, it's getting late and I don't like the door locked against Harley.'

'I'll unlock it, but first I want to say something.'

Noni felt her heart trip and drew a breath to steady it. 'What?'

'I like being with you, Noni. These last few weeks could have been hell but they haven't been. I've felt more at peace and at home than I can remember for a long time. Jacinta and I really appreciate your input.'

'I thought you were the one with the input,' she retorted naughtily.

'Behave yourself, woman.'

His finger tipped her chin up to look at him. 'You know our being together doesn't have to end when I move back to Sydney.'

Her hand clenched. For a second there she thought he was going to ask her to marry him and she didn't know what she would say. Then common sense reared its ugly head. 'I think you had better clarify that!'

'I'm asking you to come and live with me when we go back to Sydney.'

'What about Harley?'

'Well, obviously Harley has to come, too. I'm very fond of him. There's a very good school—I know, I went there. It's quite close and he could come home for weekends.'

She stiffened. 'You mean a *boarding* school? He's only five!'

Iain wasn't listening. She hated it when he did that.

He lifted his arm out from under her and his hands moved to clasp each other under the back of his head while he contemplated the ceiling. 'Your motorbike would have to go, but you wouldn't need it as you wouldn't have to work. I make more than enough money to support you. Jacinta and the baby could live with us unless she wants her own flat—but you could see to all that.'

'How useful of me.' She saw him frown at her tone of voice and she smiled grimly as she moved away to sit on the edge of her bed with her back to him. She reached down and pulled on her pyjama bottoms and then her unbuttoned top over her head.

'What a pretty little picture you've painted, Iain.

I've got another picture.' She switched on the bedside lamp and turned to face him. He blinked like an owl in the sudden light.

'How about you stay here and sell your car because I can get anything you need from the shops on my bike for you? Jacinta can go into an unmarried mother's home and visit on the weekends, and when I get home from work we can have sex when I feel like it because I'll be paying the bills.' She raised her eyebrows. 'Are you feeling flattered?'

She got up and opened the bedroom door. 'Goodnight, Iain.'

'Do you want to talk about this?'

She shook her head, not trusting herself to talk.

'Can I get dressed first?'

She gestured towards his clothes and he stood up. He held her eyes as he pulled his trousers on and slung his shirt around his shoulders.

He walked out the door without saying another word and she shut it. Firmly.

Yes, it hurt. He had as much as admitted to her that she was great fun and welcome in his bed as his lover. She didn't need to work and he would pay for Harley's private schooling. But he wouldn't marry her. Didn't love her.

She already had one child who didn't know his father. What if she had another? Iain could dictate to her and not take her seriously for the rest of her life.

More importantly, she would be cheating herself. She didn't want to regret the time she'd spent in Iain's arms. She had two options. Say goodbye and try to forget him.

Or fight for what she hoped were strong foundations to build a strong relationship with the man she loved.

Noni decided to fight. The next day was Saturday and it started off fine.

Harley made eighteen runs before being bowled out. Noni turned to Iain and inclined her head in acknowledgement. 'He's definitely improving.'

Iain smiled and dropped an arm around her shoulder while they waited for Harley to reach them.

He was looking and grinning at Iain, not Noni, but she didn't mind. The intricacies of the male sporting mind would probably always escape her. Her son looked happier, that was all that mattered.

'Well done, mate. Your mummy and I are proud of you. Your batting's getting better every week.'

Grinning, Harley looked at his mother.

'Congratulations, darling.' He even suffered a hug before wriggling free and running over to join the rest of the team.

After the game they packed up and went home. Aunt Win disappeared off to her usual haunts and Noni and Iain watched her leave from the front verandah.

'Where does she go?' Iain realised it was the first time he had wondered. He looked at Noni and she had a mischievous smile on her face. Had he said something funny?

'She's a member of a nudist colony and they have a retreat up in the foothills.' Noni turned to go inside.

She spoke over her shoulder. 'What were you planning on doing this afternoon?'

Iain blinked and tried to block out the picture that was forming of Aunt Win free to the air—then he forgot about Win and followed Noni in. He admired the taut little backside walking away from him and he was sure it was sending out come-hither vibes.

'How about a video for the offspring and we could do some more talking in your bedroom?'

'That sounds interesting. What do you suppose we could talk about?'

'No idea.' His expression belied that.

Noni shook her head. 'I know very little about you, Iain. I'd like to hear about your life away from here. Somehow I don't think I'd get to hear that if we "talked" in the bedroom.'

He gave a noncommittal nod and followed her. He wasn't sure he was ready for this.

Noni never did get to hear about Iain's pre-Burra life but he didn't get his way either. Noni was called into work to assist in an after-hours Caesarean birth, something she couldn't have done if Iain hadn't been there to mind Harley. He felt like the nanny.

It was a strange experience for Iain to see the way Noni immediately distanced herself from him as she quickly went to change into her uniform. He didn't like it.

Suddenly he wondered if that was how his wife had felt when he'd done the same for his practice. Teatime came and went, he tucked Harley into bed and Noni still wasn't home.

Iain found himself wondering if Noni needed more help.

Now, that was something he'd never thought about at a big city hospital.

He even wondered if the woman who was giving birth could be someone from the antenatal classes. The odds were shortened that you would know the person in a small community—and he was actually coming to like that concept. Before he'd come here he would have sworn he appreciated the anonymity of the city.

He was starting to miss his work—hard to imagine, but true. Ironically, he would be a more holistic obstetrician after Noni's classes. The corner of his mouth lifted as he imagined the faces on some of his colleagues.

Then he realised he still hadn't cleared up that issue of his true speciality with Noni. Even though he'd done it to avoid conflict, it had been dumb. He'd tell her the next time he saw her.

Noni didn't arrive home until almost midnight and Iain thought she looked tired. He decided to discuss it the next day.

In the early hours of Sunday morning, someone knocked on Noni's bedroom door.

'Noni, it's me, Jacinta. Can I come in?'

Noni pushed back the covers and slid out of bed, padding silently across the carpet to open the door.

Jacinta stood there with enormous eyes and a towel between her legs.

Noni's first crazy thought was, She can't, she

hasn't finished her antenatal classes. Then she laughed at herself for behaving like a nervous mother.

'Come in, sweetie. So tonight's the night.' Noni clasped Jacinta's cold hand and squeezed it.

'You'll be fine. Look, I have my little trumpet for listening to baby's heartbeat. Stand still for a moment and we'll see what he or she thinks of someone pulling the plug out of the bath.'

Noni put the fist-sized trumpet against Jacinta's round belly and closed her eyes to listen. 'Baby's head has come down well and the heartbeats sound fine.' She stood up.

'Come through and have a shower in my bathroom. I'll get your things together and wake your father. Have you any contractions yet?'

Jacinta shook her head, but she still had her lip caught between her teeth. Finally she said something. 'When do the waters stop dripping?'

'When you have the baby. You can't stop it. Just do like the cricketers do, and pad up.'

'That's disgusting, Noni.'

Noni watched her shake her head but the girl couldn't help smiling, and Noni shooed her into the bathroom, well pleased with Jacinta's state of mind.

She trod quietly up the hallway to Iain's room and pushed open the door. 'Iain?'

'Noni?' His voice was calm, as if he always had people stealing into his room in the early hours of the morning. 'Couldn't leave me alone?'

'Jacinta's waters have broken. She's in the shower in my room and I'll get her things.'

'Have you checked for cord prolapse?'

Noni frowned. There was something different in his voice. 'Don't be paranoid.'

'Don't patronise me. The head was high, and if it was a big gush, cord prolapse is a possibility.'

She raised her eyebrows. 'You're a surgeon and I'm the midwife. Since when were you an obstetrician?'

'Oh, hell, Noni. For the last nine years. Now, please, examine her.'

Noni shook her head twice as if once wouldn't clear it. 'Let me get this clear. You lied to me *twice*. You're actually an *obstetrician*?' She erased any expression from her face and spoke to his left shoulder.

'*You* examine her. The head's well down, foetal hearts are between 120 and a 140 and she's draining copious amounts of clear liquor.'

Then she looked at his face. 'I'll be there for her if she needs me until she has the baby, but I don't want to speak to you ever again. You creep!' She spun on her heel and went along to Jacinta's room to throw the last few things into the girl's bag before returning to her own room.

Iain was there when she went in and she dropped the bag in front of him.

'Noni?'

She ignored him, turned and walked out again. Then she stopped, came back, glared into his face and knocked on the bathroom door.

'Jacinta? How're you going in there?' As she listened at the door, the shower stopped. 'Here are some things to put on. Your dad is going to take you to the hospital and I'll stay here until the morning when

Aunt Win comes home, before coming up. Remember, you mightn't start having contractions until later in the day. If you need me sooner, I'll wake Harley and bring him with me. OK?'

'OK. I'm fine. Still no contractions. Tell Dad I'll be out in a minute.'

Noni looked at Iain. 'He's right here. I'm going to check on Harley.' She had to get out of there. She was going to throw something at Iain any minute now if she didn't. She sidestepped to avoid going close to him as she went past, and breathed a sigh of relief as she hit the corridor. Until he grabbed her arm.

'Get your hand off me. See to your daughter, Mr Obstetrician.' She looked down at his large hand against her paler skin and brushed it away as if it were a spider. Her voice was barely above a whisper. The coldness in her voice would have frozen a volcano.

The black brows drew together. 'Look, I know I'm in big trouble, but we don't have time for this now. I've been incredibly stupid, not explaining it all to you before now, but I didn't want to get involved in hospital politics.'

'Tell someone who cares.'

He followed her down the stairs to the kitchen and she could feel him behind her. Noni was sure there was steam coming out of her ears.

'Talk to me.'

'I can't believe it. An obstetrician. No wonder you never asked about my work. You didn't want to give yourself away. What further proof do I need that you're untrustworthy? All those discussions in the classes—you knew it all. You must have been laughing your head off.'

Iain winced. 'It seemed like a good idea at the time.'

She turned the light on in the kitchen and plugged the kettle in viciously. '"It seemed like a good idea at the time,"' she mimicked. 'So that's how you know Dr Soams, too.'

Noni gritted her teeth and squeezed all the aggressive thoughts and anger into a tiny cubicle of her brain and mentally forced the door shut on them. It was quite a battle. Then she drew in a deep breath and consciously relaxed her shoulders. Forget about him. Jacinta is the important one now.

She felt Iain's hand on her shoulder and she peeled it away from her skin again. She felt the anger bubble up again and slammed the lid shut. 'Please, keep away from me as much as you can in the circumstances.'

Her words were very clearly enunciated in a dangerously quiet voice. 'Perhaps you could put Jacinta's bag in the car. I really don't want her to have to cope with friction between the two of us.'

'Look, Noni, it's a long story and I'm sorry I misled you.'

She looked up at him and steeled herself against softening. It wasn't fair. 'When all this is over, you'd better have a bloody good explanation.'

The jug switched off and she made two mugs of tea and walked past him out of the kitchen door. She would have liked to have stomped but she'd have spilt the tea. It was the little things in life that were so frustrating.

Within half an hour Iain and Jacinta had left for the hospital. It was 4.30 a.m. Noni tidied Jacinta's room and smoothed her hand across the baby names book lying on the dresser. She refused to think about Iain and his deception or the fact that the man she loved had lied to her for weeks. Why would he do that? What else would he lie about? She shook her head and straightened her shoulders. Jacinta was the important one here.

As soon as Win came home, she would go in to work.

When Noni arrived at the hospital in her uniform, she was glad to see the ward had quietened down.

'Hi, Noni.' Cathy was on again and sat at the nurses' station, waiting for hand-over report. She grinned at her. 'I see the lodgers are in. I gather you'd like me to do the nursery while you take the birthing suite?'

'Thanks, Cath. Do you know how she's going?'

'Night staff are still with her. If you want to relieve them so they can come out, I'll give you report on the rest of the ward later.'

'Sounds good.' Noni tucked her bag into her locker and headed down the hallway. She knocked gently and pushed open the door.

Jacinta was sitting up on the bed with the baby monitor strapped to her stomach. She looked miserable. She smiled wanly at Noni who frowned at the paper hanging out of the machine. Judging by the length of it, she'd been strapped up for a while.

The night sister tilted her head towards Iain and raised her eyebrows as if to say, It's not my fault.

Noni crossed the room without looking at Iain and took Jacinta's hand. 'Hi, how're you going?'

'It hurts.'

'I know, sweetie. You'll feel better when you get up. When did the pains start?'

'About an hour ago, and they're getting stronger and closer together.' Jacinta drew in a breath and closed her eyes. 'Here comes another one.'

They all watched as Jacinta breathed slowly in and out through the pain with her eyes shut tight and her body rigid on the bed. Noni frowned and shook her head. What was she doing, strapped to the bed? The night sister wasn't a strong advocate for excessive monitoring so it had to be Iain's idea.

'Big sigh as the pain finishes, Jacinta, and then let your muscles go really floppy.' She tilted her head and watched as the girl tried to relax. 'Drop your shoulders. Good. Let's get you off this bed. How would you like a nice hot shower?'

Iain stepped forward but Noni didn't give him a chance to speak. 'What a lovely tracing of Baby's heartbeat. We can take that off now we can see how happy Baby is in there. Look at all these contraction hills we've recorded.'

She looked at him from under her brows. 'You're happy with this, aren't you, Iain?'

He looked back at her the same way and nodded his head. 'As you say, a healthy trace.'

The night sister made a strangled noise and squeezed her lips together to stop the grin. 'Jacinta started contracting at 5.30 and Dr McCloud was concerned. I'll leave you to carry on here, Noni, and give my report to Cathy. Good luck, Jacinta. Bye, everybody.'

'Thanks, Rae.' Jacinta smiled wanly as the other midwife left the room. Iain leaned against the wall and watched Noni with his eyes narrowed.

'OK, sweetie, let's get these belts off your tummy and you into the shower.'

They shuffled their way into the chair in the shower and Jacinta leaned her head against the wall as Noni directed the hot water over her back. 'That feels wonderful.' Noni showed her how to change the direction of the spray.

'Keep the nozzle of the hand shower over the part where the pain is during contractions and the heat will help.' She draped a towel around Jacinta's shoulders to stop her getting cold. 'I'm just ducking out here for a moment to talk to your father.'

'I'll be fine.'

Noni leaned forward and brushed the hair out of the girl's eyes. 'I know you will. You're doing beautifully. And you're designed to do it.'

Jacinta chorused the last line and they smiled at each other.

'I'll be back soon.' Noni shut the bathroom door behind her and moved over to where Iain was leaning on the wall.

'We're both glad to see you, although I won't allow

you to steamroller me all the time.' His voice was quiet but firm.

'I never thought you would. Jacinta needs you to stop thinking like an obstetrician—' she tried not to put an inflection on the word '—and more like a support person. You aren't dealing with the usual high-risk pregnancy you'd be called in for. She's a perfectly healthy young woman with a healthy baby. Excessive monitoring of normal labour can cause complications, because people can't help interfering—you know that.'

'OK.' He put his hand up. 'I'll go home and shower and be back in an hour. Phone me if you need me earlier.'

She watched him go, and even though she was still angry with him for his deception she acknowledged his fear of something going wrong for Jacinta. Well, negative people shouldn't be in the birthing suite and she believed everything was going to go beautifully. She had to.

'How's it going, Jacinta?' The bathroom was steamy and Noni carried some ice chips over to the shower. 'Suck on these between contractions and I'll put a cold washcloth on the rail in case you feel faint from the heat.'

'They're getting really strong, Noni.' Noni could hear the first flutters of panic in Jacinta's voice.

'I know, sweetie, but remember they are all good pains. When you get one I want you to imagine your baby's head being pushed into the neck of your uterus and the cervix opening bit by bit. Every pain brings you closer to meeting your baby and you want to be as loose as you can be to let the muscles do their work.' She massaged the girl's shoulders and was rewarded by the sudden dropping of her shoulders as she relaxed.

'After a while, when the shower isn't helping any more, what should you do?'

'Change positions and do something else.' By half an hour later, Jacinta's voice was starting to sound sleepy as she rested her head on her arms against the rail. She was groaning freely but hardly tensed her muscles now as the contractions rolled over her. Noni was careful not to disturb her during the concentration of coping with the pain, and she marvelled again at how women could fall into a state of almost dozing between the contractions as the body's natural endorphins kicked in.

Noni heard the other door open. Iain was back.

CHAPTER NINE

JACINTA'S moans carried clearly through the door and Iain's face blanched.

'She's in pain. Listen to her groaning. For God's sake, give her some pain relief. What about an epidural?'

'For you or for her?' Noni rested her hand on his arm. 'She's coping and she's in strong labour. If she can't stand it she'll ask for something, but I believe she's progressing very quickly.'

'Have you checked her progress?'

Noni sighed. 'Why? So that we won't have to wonder how far she is? Is that more important than her staying undisturbed in the shower to get on with it? For goodness' sake, at least wait for a sign. Something will happen that indicates progress. Baby's heart rate is fine—I listen to it every fifteen minutes for a minute. She hasn't asked for pain relief, the contractions are regular and two- to three-minutely.' She looked into his face. 'Let her be, Iain.'

He wiped his forehead. 'She'd better not have that baby in the bathroom.'

'Really? I thought she could have the baby wherever she wants to have it.'

'You're joking!'

She could see that really rattled him. She smiled at him. 'Come in and sit with us.'

139

Noni rested her hand on the girl's shoulder. 'Jacinta, your father's back.'

'Hi, Dad.' Her voice seemed to come from far away.

'Hi, Jaz. How're you going?'

She groaned in reply as another pain rolled over her. When it was finished, Noni watched Iain loosen his clenched hands. He looked like he wouldn't be able to take much more of this.

'I'm OK.' The sleepy voice startled him as Jacinta finished the conversation as if she'd never stopped it to groan.

Noni grinned and stepped back from where she was rubbing Jacinta's back. 'Why don't you rub for a while and I'll get some more ice?' She gestured for him to change positions with her. 'You've probably never participated in this side of obstetrics before. Try to remember the concepts from the antenatal classes.'

She watched him rub firmly when Jacinta groaned and gently when she relaxed between them. Noni smiled at Iain's expensive shoes being ruined by the water. She'd told him in class to bring wet-weather gear. She just nodded and left them to it.

By twelve-thirty, they'd been in and out of the shower three times and lost count of the times they'd walked the length of the ward. Jacinta was getting agitated and Iain was looking tortured. She could see—for him—this was nothing like being the consultant who came and went a couple of times during his patient's labour.

Jacinta was sitting on the birthing stool, leaning

back against the shower-recess wall. The hand-held shower nozzle sprayed Iain's shoes when Jacinta's pain was at its height. The pains were coming hard and fast. Iain was looking grimmer by the minute.

Jacinta gave a strange, strangled scream and Iain jumped. He couldn't stand it any more.

'That's it.' He brought his face down next to Noni's. 'I'm not putting her through any more of this. Get her an epidural.'

Noni raised her eyebrows. 'If that's what she wants, of course I can arrange that. But my instincts tell me she's going through transition. She's almost in second stage. Are you sure it's Jacinta who can't stand it?'

'Get it!'

Noni turned her back on him. 'Jacinta? How are you going?'

'I want to go home.' She wailed. 'I don't want to do this any more. Daddy, help me...'

Iain took her hand and glared at Noni. 'It's OK, baby. We're getting you an epidural.'

'Ooh-h.'

'I don't think so.' Noni was smiling and Iain couldn't believe his ears.

'Are you mad? That's an order.'

'Well, she'll have to wait until after the baby is born, then, Doctor, if I'm not mistaken.' She crouched down beside the girl. 'What were you feeling with that last pain?'

'I want to push. I have to go to the toilet. Get me up from here.'

'OK, sweetie. It's OK. This is the part we talked

about, where we can finally do something with the pain. Up you come and I'll come with you while you sit on the toilet.'

The next sixty minutes were hell for Iain. As far as he could tell, Noni saw nothing wrong with it. When Jacinta complained about the pain, she agreed.

'I know it's hard, sweetie. That sharp, burning pain that feels like a knife is where your body is telling you to push.'

Jacinta grunted and groaned her way through the contraction.

'It's not working. Why is it so slow?' she said through gritted teeth.

'Everything is stretching to make way for the baby. You're doing beautifully. You don't want it to pop out—you want your baby to ease out gently.' Noni wiped the beads of perspiration off Jacinta's brow with a washcloth dipped in icy water.

Jacinta threw her head up and glared at them. 'Drink!'

Noni smiled at the economical request. 'We're getting down to serious business here.'

'Don't you think we should move her onto the bed?' Iain looked to be gauging if he could carry his daughter out of the bathroom.

Noni raised one eyebrow quizzically but didn't answer.

Iain finally realised that Noni was quite content to have his grandchild born in the shower. 'Jacinta, baby, I think you should get up now and come and lie on the bed.'

'I'm not going anywhere. Noni, it *hur-rts*.'

Another huge push later, the first crescent of black hair could be seen.

Noni reached behind her and picked up a mirror. She propped it in front of Jacinta. 'Have a look, Jaz. See the baby's head.'

Jacinta glanced up from where she was concentrating on the floor and suddenly she saw it. 'It's got black hair.' With eyes glued to the progress she could see, she bore down with gritted teeth.

'For God's sake, where's Soams?'

The bathroom door opened. 'I'm here, Iain. Looks like you three have been swimming.' The older doctor looked across at Noni with a twinkle in his eye. 'Do you need me, Sister?'

Noni smiled and shook her head before concentrating on the girl in front of her. 'OK, Jaz. Slow it down. Gentle now, and pant. Little pushes. Good girl.' Her gloved hand hovered under the baby's head without touching it. 'Lovely.'

Iain had been having the worst hour of his life. Then it changed.

He watched his grandchild's head finally being born, soon followed by the anterior shoulder and then the other shoulder.

'Reach down and slip your fingers under Baby's armpits.'

Jacinta's hands came tentatively down to touch her child, and with a final push Baby slithered out into Noni's hands. Jacinta automatically lifted her child to her chest and cradled her.

Iain couldn't believe the strain and stress was over.

He'd never felt so weary in his life. He brushed away the moisture from his eyes and met Noni's smile across the bathroom floor. He didn't say the words but mouthed them clearly enough for her to understand. 'Nice delivery.' She glared at him, as he'd known she would.

'Congratulations, Jacinta. It's a girl.' Dr Soams chuckled as Noni placed a warm bunny rug over mother and daughter to help Jacinta keep the slippery infant against her. She stared at the tiny screwed-up face and then tentatively kissed her baby.

'It's over. I did it. A daughter.' She let her breath out in a big sigh.

Then she looked up at Noni and her father. 'What are you two crying about?' She gathered the little scrap closer to her chest. 'You're going to have to go through this one day, kid. But it's worth it.'

Noni looked at Iain as Dr Soams declared, 'Jacinta looks a hundred per cent, compared to her father. You look like you've been run over by a truck, Iain.' Noni stifled a laugh—so much for the *obstetrician*.

It was almost three o'clock in the afternoon. 'What a beautiful picture—mother and baby tucked up in bed together.' Noni smiled at Jacinta's dreamy expression. The girl was gazing adoringly at her tiny daughter's face.

'Isn't Olivia lovely?'

'Yes, she is. I'm nearly ready to head home, Jacinta. Do you need help with anything before I go?'

'No, thanks, Noni. Breastfeeding isn't so bad. It

just felt right when she was born for her to be there at my breast.'

'Sometimes it happens like that for people who think they want to formula-feed. As long as you're happy, I think it's wonderful. And Olivia knows what she wants—just like her mother.'

'I can't believe it's all over and she's mine.' Jacinta stroked the tiny palm until Olivia's fingers curled and grasped her mother's larger one. She smiled at Noni. 'When's Aunt Win and Harley coming in?'

'They'll be up after tea when you've had a rest, but something tells me you won't be sleeping— you're too excited. You're a very clever girl.' She leaned over and kissed them both on the cheek.

'Your father will probably be in before us tonight. Bye, Jaz.'

Noni scooped up her bag from beside the bed and waved as she headed for the door.

When she arrived home, Iain was sitting on the back verandah.

'Congratulations, Grandpa.' She gave him a plastic smile, almost amused that he looked startled she was talking to him. *Keep trying to figure me out, buster.* She didn't stop, and pushed through the door. 'Aunt Win?'

She heard Iain follow her in.

'She said she'd be back soon. She's gone to buy something pink for the baby. So you'll have to talk to me.'

Noni smiled sweetly at him. 'I don't have to do anything, Doctor.'

'No, you don't. But I would like you to at least

give me a chance to say thank you.' He turned her to face him.

The feel of his arms made her traitorous body want to step closer, but she supposed she'd have to get used to that and not give in.

'You're very good at what you do, Noni. I learnt a lot today and Jacinta and I are really glad you were there.'

She hated that. The sleaze. It was so much easier if she could just keep being cold with him. She could feel herself weakening again.

'I was glad to be there and Jacinta was fabulous. But Harley will be back from school in a minute and I want to have a shower before he gets home.'

Noni took the stairs two at a time without looking back, but she could feel his eyes on her. That had been close. She'd really wanted to throw herself into his arms but some time during the day she'd realised it wasn't going to work. He wasn't going to commit himself fully to her and she was going to do it right this time. She and Harley couldn't afford to get hurt.

The hot needles of spray soothed away the tensions of the night and morning. As Noni slowly rotated under the shower she accepted they didn't have a two-sided relationship. She had been building hope onto something that just wasn't there. Iain hadn't promised her anything concrete so it was no use complaining he'd misled her.

Imagine if she'd taken Harley out of school and moved to Sydney with Iain. Then if she'd found out how little she meant to him... She shuddered. She wouldn't be making that mistake again.

She turned the shower off and stepped out, thoughts tumbling around in her mind. Iain and Jacinta would be gone by this time next week. All I have to do is distance myself from Iain and start preparing Harley for their departure, she decided. Noni sighed. If only it were that easy.

At the hospital later that evening, after Win and Harley had left, Noni felt exhausted from trying not to catch Iain's eye. They sat opposite each other across Jacinta's bed. She gave up and rose from the chair to make her own departure.

'I'll leave you with your dad, Jacinta, and see you tomorrow when I come to work.'

'Noni, before you leave. What happens when I leave the hospital?' Jacinta looked straight at her father. 'When were you planning to go back to Sydney, Dad?'

Iain shifted in his seat. 'I expect we'll go back Saturday, once you feel up to travelling.'

Noni had known it was coming, but hearing it stated as a fact hit her like a blow to her chest.

Noni looked away from Jacinta but knew the girl had seen her distress. She gathered her bag, ostensibly to search for her keys, and moistened her lips. She gripped the keys as if someone were threatening to take them off her, and the pain from the metal teeth digging into her hands felt strangely appropriate.

'You two will sort it out. I have to go. Goodnight.' She waved without meeting their eyes and turned away.

*   *   *

Noni avoided Iain as much as living in the same house allowed her to while Jacinta was in the hospital. It was harder when the girl came home as everyone gravitated towards mother and baby when they had a spare minute. Noni's face felt stiff from hiding how she felt from Jacinta and Harley.

Friday arrived. The good news had been that a temporary replacement obstetrician had agreed to do a three-month stint at Burra while a last-ditch recruitment drive was carried out. Work had been busy as usual and she was almost glad to be home. Despite Iain being there.

She sat on the chair outside the kitchen window to slip her shoes off and was wriggling her toes still trapped inside her pantihosed feet.

Jacinta pushed open the screen door and sat down next to her. 'Noni? Can I come to classes with you tonight, and show off Olivia?'

'It's the last night. You just want to come for the food.' She grinned. 'Of course you can. I'm sure everyone would love to see both of you. You sure you're not too tired?'

'I've been home two days and Olivia's only woken once for a night feed. I reckon I'm almost back to my pre-pregnant self.'

'Fine. Just remember everyone is going to ask you about the labour.'

'Not the gory bits?'

Noni laughed. 'Especially the gory bits.'

Jacinta shrugged. 'I just won't tell them stuff if I don't want to.'

Noni smiled to herself, stood up and patted the

younger woman on the shoulder. 'Keep that strength. I know I won't have to worry about you. You'll handle anything life throws at you.'

Jacinta screwed her face up and rolled her eyes. 'Yeah, right.' She raised her hand. 'Noni, before you go...'

Noni stopped with one hand on the screen door.

'What are you doing about your relationship with Dad?'

Noni felt her face stiffen again. She thought of launching into a big explanation. She thought of saying, I haven't decided. Then she looked at the no-nonsense face of the woman in front of her. What *could* she do about a man who didn't need her in his life?

Get on with her own.

'Nothing.' She grimaced and looked at the floor. She pulled the door open again and stepped inside, straight into the arms of the man she'd just given up on.

His arms tightened around her for a moment before they fell away. They both stepped back and Noni nearly fell through the screen door again. Iain caught her shoulder to balance her and this time his hand took longer to let go.

Noni closed her eyes briefly before gently loosening his fingers to sweep his hand off her shoulder.

'Thank you,' she said stiffly, and moved past him into the house. She hated that. Why did she have to be the one who almost fell over? It should have been him. Maybe because if the positions had been reversed, she would have let him drop.

*   *   *

When Noni came downstairs ready to head out to the class, Iain was standing in the hallway.

'Do you mind if I come with you?' he asked.

Noni shrugged fatalistically. 'They're your classes too, although it would have been a courtesy if you'd mentioned your profession.'

'I've apologised for that.'

Noni felt like screaming. 'I don't really want to rehash anything, Iain. So don't wallow in it. You're the one who wants to live on the surface of life. Just let me go to my class and do my job.'

He didn't say anything, just stared at her thoughtfully until she turned away.

'Is Jacinta ready?'

'We'll take my car.'

She snorted and raised her eyebrows. 'Will you?'

'We'll all go in my car.'

She picked up her helmet. 'Right.' She pushed open the screen and strode off to get her motorbike.

When she unlocked the door to the group room she threw the keys on the table. At least she had ten minutes to herself before they arrived. She slammed open a couple of windows and rearranged chairs with aggressive precision. By the time the room was organised, she felt better. People started to arrive.

Paul and Suzie shuffled in, and Suzie was holding her stomach.

Noni raised her eyebrows. 'Having a few pains, you two?'

Suzie breathed out and let go of her stomach. 'They've been coming and going for a few days now.

I've still got three weeks to go and it's driving me crazy. Paul keeps trying to shove me into the car to come to the hospital. Talk some sense into him, Noni.'

'He's just trying to do the right thing.'

Paul looked nervous and Noni remembered the feeling of not knowing when labour was ready to really kick in.

'She'll know when she's ready, Paul. It could take days or even weeks for labour to truly start. You'll drive each other crazy if you worry all the time.'

They both looked dejected at that, and Noni tilted her head in sympathy.

'Some people get these pains for ages beforehand—but the good news is it usually speeds up the true labour when it does arrive.' She spoke to Paul. 'It's your job to keep the car filled up with petrol for a quick getaway when the time finally arrives.'

Paul ran his hand over his chin. 'Well can I have one of those cord clamp things? I'm sure Junior's going to pop his head out as we go over the traffic bridge, and then where will we be?'

Noni laughed. 'On the right side of the river, but I know what you mean. It's a worry.' She smiled at Suzie. 'Have faith. She'll know when you need to hit the road. Just wait for her.'

More people arrived and Noni smiled and welcomed them. Finally everyone was assembled.

'As you can see, we've had our first baby.' The prospective mothers and fathers oohed and ahhed, much to Jacinta's satisfaction.

'Olivia was born on Monday and I thought we'd

ask Jacinta to describe her memories of labour while
I draw a timeline on the board. It's a kind of revision
for the classes. OK, Jacinta?' The girl nodded.

As Jacinta recounted her own memories, Noni
marked the times of changes, progress and options
used to gain pain relief on the board. Noni couldn't
help noticing Iain's pensiveness.

It appeared his own memories were different to
Jacinta's perspective on things. She wondered if the
whole experience would make him a better obstetrician in the future.

She'd never know. Special moments they'd spent
together flashed in front of her eyes. Her throat closed
over and she swallowed. Somehow she'd get through
the evening.

The snap of the lock at the last window had an air of
finality about it. Would this be her last class here? If
the maternity unit eventually shut she supposed they
could still run classes, except that the families would
have to go to the bigger hospitals to actually give
birth.

Maybe the new doctor would fall in love with the
place and stay. Although there had been some talk at
work today that he might be going to pull out.
'You're dreamin', girl,' she muttered.

'What are you dreaming about?'

She hated that. Why couldn't the guy cough or
something? Noni's indrawn breath seemed to go on
for ever. 'Well, Iain, it wasn't you.' She stopped and
frowned. 'Though it could have been now that you're
an obstetrician.'

It was his turn to frown. 'I don't understand you.'

Noni gave him a perfunctory smile as she brushed past him. 'So what's new? Goodnight.' She deliberately didn't wait to lock the door.

One thing about Iain, he wouldn't follow her until he'd ensured the place was shut properly and the lights were off. She didn't want to marry someone like that anyway.

Jacinta was sitting in the car and Noni waved before she pulled her helmet on. She didn't know why but there was an urgency to get out onto the road before Iain caught up with her. The engine roared to life just as he walked up beside the bike. He said something but she pointed to her helmet and revved the bike noisily again before she smiled evilly and accelerated away from him.

It felt good for the first twenty seconds and then her mood flattened again. She pulled up beside the beach and allowed a minute of self-pity to wash over her like the waves that slid up and over the half-submerged rocks.

She wished she'd never met Iain McCloud. She gave a half laugh, half sob. That wasn't true. He'd been a window to a place where there was more to life than being a mother, a niece and a midwife. Shame he'd shut the window. And pulled the blinds.

She started the bike again. It was no use staying here to mope.

When Noni got home Iain was on the phone. He looked serious and she felt her stomach sink. No more crises tonight, please, she prayed.

She went in search of her aunt. 'I'm going to see

Harley and then I'm off to bed. Do you know what time they're leaving tomorrow?'

Her aunt looked at her worriedly. 'They may not be leaving yet. Dr Soams has rung a few times and asked Iain to fill the three-month gap while they try to find the new O and G man. Apparently the one they'd lined up can't come. Iain must be considering it. He asked if they could continue to stay here.' She glanced at her niece's face. 'I could say no if that would be easier for you.'

'And have Harley never speak to me again?' Noni bit her lip. 'At least someone will be happy.' She patted her aunt. 'It's OK, I'll stop being a martyr soon.' She'd see Iain tomorrow at breakfast and that would be soon enough to know if the torture was going to continue.

CHAPTER TEN

'I'M STAYING for another two weeks.' Iain was looking at Noni as he passed the marmalade, but she refused to meet his eyes.

'Great.' Hell, she thought. 'I'm going out.'

'Stay.' He laid his fingers over her arm. 'I need to talk to you, Noni.'

'Well, I don't think I want to listen.' She glanced down at her arm and hated the frissons of awareness he could transmit with that light hold. She was a basket case. How was she supposed to last another fortnight?

'Jacinta said she'd mind Harley if you and I go out this afternoon. I'd really like to speak to you somewhere we won't be interrupted.'

'Why would that be, Iain?' This time she did meet his eyes and what she saw there confused her even more. She didn't think she could ride this roller-coaster much longer.

'Come and find out. Let's drive somewhere and go for a walk. We need to talk.'

It was a glorious autumn afternoon down by the river. The weeping willows swept the water's edge in places, and Iain and Noni meandered in and out beside the bank. It was Noni's favourite spot for thinking, and as usual there wasn't a soul around. It felt strange to be with Iain somewhere not related to either their children or work.

Noni had thrown a blanket and some nibbles into a bag, along with the Thermos, and Iain had just put everything down in a pile under a gum tree. They stood for a while, throwing rocks into the river, a game that started out as desultory and ended up competitive.

'Hey, that splashed me.' Iain was grinning and Noni narrowed her eyes and retaliated.

He raised his eyebrows and picked up another handful.

'Enough!' Noni laughed and stepped back to wipe the droplets of water from her face.

'So what do you want to talk to me about, Iain?'

'Can we sit down first? Please.' He held out his hand.

She stared at his long, tapered fingers before placing her own in his care. He squeezed her hand gently and smiled, and she felt as if she were being wrapped in velvet. Noni couldn't smile back but strangely couldn't look away from his face either. She'd never had that sensation before. It was as if they had both just discovered the other person.

They walked slowly, careful not to trip without watching their steps, before halting beside the trunk of a tree.

'I'll spread out the rug, shall I?' She looked down at their hands, not willing to be the first to disengage.

'I suppose I'll have to let you go.' Iain's voice was deeper than usual and she nodded her head, strangely reluctant to agree.

'It's there—isn't it, Noni? It's not just me feeling something between us when we touch?' He stroked his thumb down the edge of her hand and she turned her head to watch the goose-bumps rise on her arm.

She bit her lip. 'Maybe that's our problem.' She looked up at him and his eyes were warm and caring, like a pot of melted chocolate. 'Should we go with our feelings instead of talking about it, Iain?'

'Let's try. Come here.'

She moved to stand in the circle of his arms, rested her cheek against his shirt and closed her eyes. When he wrapped his arms around her she sighed and listened to his heart thumping. Why did she feel that his heart was the one she was destined to beat in time to? Why did she feel suddenly safe when previously safety had never been an issue? They had spent—or wasted—so much time at conversational cross-purposes. Was it really so simple?

'Do many people come along here?' Iain asked quietly.

Noni's cheeks warmed and she felt about sixteen again.

'Are you propositioning me?'

He raised those eyebrows. 'I would like to kiss you but perhaps we should go somewhere less exposed.'

'It's not a popular place, because of the stinging nettles, but we can watch out for it.'

'Stinging nettles? You're kidding!'

She pulled him along behind the tree a little way until she found a small hollow free of nettles. It was screened from the path and golden shafts of sunlight from the canopy above danced and flickered on the ground.

'Are you fond of nymphs and satyrs, Iain?' The comment was a light one but after it had been said she couldn't help her own erotic thoughts. She bit back her smile at the mental picture of Iain with horns and a tail.

'I'm uneducated there, I'm afraid, but I have my own elf to protect me. The country can be uncomfortable for us city dwellers, but I'll trust you not to expose me to pain.'

'I'll make no promises.' Their eyes met again and the undercurrents were understood. She spread the rug and stepped onto it, holding out her hand.

'Welcome to my fairy grotto. Do you dare to enter?'

'I love a dare,' he said, and took her hand.

There it was again. She could almost feel his power seeping up her arm. When he knelt and pulled her down to join him, it seemed natural to lie down with him there, under the trees.

His first kiss was like a gentle feather and brushed her lips in a breath. She sighed and nestled closer, curling her arm around his neck to pull him closer.

'You drive me crazy, elf. Or should that be fairy princess?' His eyes were staring into hers and she could see herself reflected in them.

'Stop talking and kiss me,' she demanded softly, and he chuckled before claiming her mouth to meet her needs—and his.

The kiss was slow and deep, an erotic duel of two opposing forces finding common ground. It moved to a faster pace that demanded more passion and fed upon itself. The trees were gone, the river was gone, and the world was gone in a gliding, swooping maelstrom of hunger and need and the slaking of both.

That kiss filled her body with fierce longings, her mind with swirling sensations and her spirit with a strange freedom.

Just when it wasn't enough Noni couldn't tell, but her hands were seeking to feel and mould and knead the strong body beside her. She savoured the strength of his neck and shoulders, the solid bulge of his upper arms and the strong swell of his chest.

His hands roved, too, and everywhere he touched seemed to ignite into flames. As one, their hands stilled, and a long, burning look passed between them.

'Are you sure?' he queried gently.

It could be the last time they ever made love. More sure than she would ever be in her life as long as...

'Are you prepared?' Her answer made him smile and pat his wallet.

'Undress for me, Noni. You are all this glade needs to be perfect.'

She slipped her dress over her head and leaned forward to unclasp her bra.

His indrawn breath raised her head, and she smiled at the awe in his eyes. He made her feel like the princess he'd spoken of. She didn't recognise herself as this wanton forest dweller and the illicitness of the setting seemed to insulate her from any awkwardness. She sat back on her heels and waited for him, but he was too slow. She could feel the air on her skin and she raised her eyes to the sky. This was crazy, bizarre and wonderful, and she'd never regret it.

Noni leaned forward and touched his shirt and trousers. 'Lose them. I want to see you, too, Iain.'

He shed his clothes quickly and it was her turn to stare. She ran her finger down the middle of his chest, and his quick breathing made her finger rise and fall.

He pulled her gently into his arms as they lay down and their lips met. She revelled in the hardness of his body against hers, and pressed closer until his kiss and caresses drove all thought from her mind. They rubbed their bodies against each other until every nerve ending was aching for fulfilment.

She cried out beneath the trees and tears glistened on her lashes from the beauty of it. Afterwards they lay side by side and dozed for a while until Noni began to notice the twigs and small stones only partially shielded by the blanket. His eyes were half-closed as he watched her start to fidget.

'Iain?'

'Hmm?'

'This bed has suddenly become quite lumpy.'

Iain half laughed and rolled onto his back to pull her on top of him. 'Let me look at you.' He ran his hands up the sides of her face and cupped her cheeks. 'You are incredible.'

She stared down at this man who had entered her life with such impact. Yes, she loved him. Probably would always love him. They should be able to work things out. She didn't want to think further than that.

He slid his hand behind her neck and pulled her face down to his for a swift kiss. 'Perhaps we should get dressed, and devour some of that food instead of each other,' she suggested.

'Sounds good. Where did I throw my underpants?' She started to giggle. She rested her cheek on his chest and laughed into his chin. Iain closed his eyes in mock exasperation.

'Where are your words of awe, woman? That was pretty darned wonderful and you're laughing.'

Noni hiccoughed, kissed his chin and unfolded herself from on top of him to stand.

They dressed quickly and stepped out from the shelter of the trees. Noni reopened the blanket in a patch of late afternoon sunlight and unpacked the hamper.

They ate, leaning against each other and staring at the ripples in the water. Finally Iain started to talk.

'I don't want to go back to Sydney without you, Noni.'

So it had come. He did want her with him. But on what terms? Noni waited for her heartbeat to settle back to normal. How easy it would be just to say yes, and not worry about the future or the lies or the risk. They had made love, twice, and it was hard to imagine Iain not being there, but she had more to fight for.

'I've lived in the same house with you for the last six weeks and I still know very little about you. I could live with you for a year and still not know you.'

'What do you want to know?'

'Lots of things.'

'Shoot.'

'Why you lied to me for a start. I'd like you to explain your reasons for keeping me at a distance. I'd like to know where you met Jacinta's mother and I'd like to know about your family.' Now that she'd started she found it hard to stop.

He reached out and lifted her fingers to rest them in his palm.

'All of that, and more, eh?' He raised his eyebrows. 'Well, I'm not particularly proud of the deceptions about my job—but that's all part of my defence against a particular blonde-haired mini-bombshell that I was trying to stop myself from racing off with.'

He grimaced. 'Here I was, finally meeting my commitment to my long-lost daughter, and there you were, distracting me. It was very disconcerting. Then there was the hospital staff shortage and I wanted to avoid a situation where you knew I was an obstetrician—but still couldn't help you. To lie to you was wrong, to do it twice was lunacy—and I'm sorry. I guess it's true that one lie leads to another.'

He sighed. 'As for keeping you at a distance—again, that was self-protection. I haven't had much long-term success with the women in my life. And most of it has been my fault.'

She tilted her head and looked at him quizzically. 'This doesn't sound like the Iain I know.'

'As you said before, you don't know me well. Perhaps I'm afraid that if you did know me you might not like what you see.'

Noni shook her head at that. 'Tell me about your childhood.'

'What's there to tell? My father walked out and left me with my mother when I was very young.' He twisted a blade of grass between his fingers. 'I vowed

I would never do to my children what he did to me. But it seems I did.'

Noni felt his pain. 'You didn't know about Jacinta.'

It was his turn to shake his head. 'That doesn't make it right.'

'Tell me about your mother.'

He looked up. 'I didn't understand my mother. She was a very bitter woman. I had quite a few ''uncles'' who didn't stay in the picture long, and I don't think I learned how to have a long-lasting relationship. The ones I did try were a dismal failure.'

He ticked them off his fingers. 'Jacinta's mother. Well, I was young. Twenty-one, my mother still alive, and I was about to dive into my medical training when I met Adele. She wasn't the daughter-in-law my mother had planned. Also, she was five years older than I was.

'Adele was a stunningly beautiful woman and I think she was amused that I had fallen for her. I can see now I was infatuated with her. I asked her to marry me numerous times during that crazy month, but she always refused.'

He took a sip of his coffee. 'Then one day she changed. It was as if she couldn't stand the sight of me and eventually I stopped trying to see her. She gave me the impression she had a new lover, although I never heard of anyone with her. Obviously, now, I realise she was pregnant. Not long after that I moved away. I met my wife, Wendy, a nurse at King George Hospital, and we were married in haste to repent at leisure. The ironic part about it was that my wife and I were unable to have children. It's hard not to wonder if our marriage would have been different if Adele had told us of Jacinta's birth.'

He stared into the empty cup.

Noni squeezed his other hand. 'Perhaps Adele felt it would have tied her to a man she had nothing in common with.'

He looked up sharply. 'Are you condoning her behaviour?' His voice was clipped but she didn't care.

Noni shot back at him. 'Are you damning her without knowing the full story?'

They glared at each other across the rug. How had they got into this after what they had just been through? It was almost as if Noni was on a self-destruct mission. She should be steering the conversation away from this topic. Or she could just get it out in the open.

Iain was on a different track. 'So are you coming to Sydney with me or not?'

Talking just didn't work for them. But she had to clear the air before they went further. 'That's a big ask, Iain. I don't think it would work. There are so many things we still don't know about each other.'

'Like what?'

'You've never asked about Harley's father.'

Iain sat back. He didn't think he wanted to know. 'I guess I assumed he was dead.'

'Well, you assumed wrong. He was a one-night stand.' She met his eyes. 'I never told him about Harley, just like Adele never told you.'

Iain couldn't believe what he was hearing.

'So there's some guy out there who could waltz into your life and claim half your son.' And claim

Noni, too. If she'd fancied him once she could do so again. He felt the cold seep into his body as if someone had opened the freezer door. He definitely didn't want to hear this.

'No. That wouldn't happen.'

'How can you be so sure?'

'Because even if I did know where he was, I wouldn't tell him.'

Iain winced. Just like Adele. It all rose up in front of him, all the pain he'd felt at his exclusion from Jacinta's younger years. He'd picked the wrong one again. There was no future for him and Noni.

He tried to stamp down his bitterness but it rose in his throat. 'What if something goes wrong for you, like it did for Adele? Are you going to dump Harley in his lap out of the blue?'

Noni stood up and splashed the contents of her own cup onto the grass. 'You don't want to hear my side, do you?' She gathered up the rest of the picnic and shoved it willy-nilly in the bag.

'You're not perfect. You don't want to get involved, do you, Iain? You're willing to offer me a temporary arrangement because that's convenient for you. It's safe and if it doesn't work out then you can blame your mother for not teaching you about long-term relationships.' She snorted.

'This way you're not compelled to take the tough times with the smooth. Don't you know that the more you put into a relationship the more you'll get out of it?'

She picked up her bag. 'Well, that's no better than trapping the man who was Harley's father. He wasn't interested in a relationship with me, and I'm not interested in one with you. I'd really prefer if you'd find somewhere else to stay for the next fortnight until you go back to where you came from.'

'But I'm still allowed to work the next two weeks to save your precious maternity ward,' Iain said cynically as he rose from the blanket.

Noni turned and started to walk back to the car.

When Suzie and Paul went in to have their baby, they couldn't believe their luck.

'Imagine Iain being the doctor on call and you the midwife. That's great.' Paul was grinning.

Noni smiled weakly and ushered them into the birthing suite. The last fortnight had been horrendous. Iain and Jacinta had moved to Dr Soams's house and the whole hospital was talking about a possible relationship and split between Iain and Noni. The rumours she'd tracked back to Penelope Soams.

The worst part was Iain was being so damn nice. His smile warmed her undisciplined heart and she acknowledged how well he adapted to the more holistic care Burra provided for their maternity patients.

Surprisingly, he was finally giving her his full attention whenever she had to speak to him. She had the feeling it was all a strategic game but she couldn't figure out the rules. He made no effort to discuss any of the personal issues they'd disagreed on, or even tried to see her out of work hours. Not that she would have gone. She kept telling herself it would be over soon if the tension didn't kill her.

It was harder to work together than to live in the

same house. If Noni had to have another polite conversation with Iain McCloud she would scream. At least Suzie's labour passed quickly and kept her mind occupied.

Noni had completed an examination and then sponged the woman's face after a particularly strong contraction. 'Now we have time to tell you. You're eight centimetres dilated, your cervix is very thin and almost ready to open all the way.'

Suzie looked up with the first threads of panic in her eyes. 'I don't know if I'm ready to do this.' She reached for her husband's hand. 'I thought I'd have the baby late tonight as it's my first child.'

Paul squeezed her hand back. 'Remember transition and the "frantic" feelings Noni talked about? That might be what you're feeling now.'

Noni nodded. 'I think so, too, and this is the first time I've had someone complain about their labour being over too soon.' She laid her hand on Suzie's arm and smiled reassuringly. 'It was all that practice your uterus had before coming into labour. That annoying stopping and starting has done great things.'

'Nice to know it had an upside.' Paul looked more exhausted than his wife did. 'We haven't had a decent night's sleep for weeks.'

'You'll both probably be too excited to sleep tonight.'

'Here comes another one. Ooh.' Suzie hunched forward on the birth ball and Paul rubbed the small of her back in a slow, circular motion.

'You guys are doing brilliantly. I'll give Iain a ring and let him know how you're going.'

Noni closed the door behind her and leaned back on it. She sighed to relax her shoulders before straightening up and pushing herself off the door. She had to force herself to go to the desk and pick up the phone.

'Dr Soams's and Dr McCloud's surgery. Hold the line, please.' Penelope's voice grated on Noni's ears and she rolled her eyes as she waited.

'Can I help you?'

'It's Sister Frost. Can I speak to Dr McCloud, please?' Noni's voice was brisk and she acknowledged that she didn't feel this way with any of the other doctors' secretaries. She really should get over this.

'Dr McCloud speaking.'

Noni watched the hairs on her arms rise, and closed her eyes. How could he do that to her with just his voice? She realised she hadn't answered and opened her eyes. 'It's Noni.'

'Noni. What can I do for you?' His voice softened and her mind threatened to wander again before she pulled herself up smartly.

'Suzie and Paul are in labour here, and chugging along at eight centimetres. The baby's head is fairly low in her pelvis. I don't think you'd better hang around when I ring to say she's in second stage.'

'Foetal heart's fine?'

'Yes, Doctor.' Why wouldn't it be? He was so tuned for disaster it drove her crazy. That wasn't the only thing driving her crazy.

'I'll see you soon, then.'

But soon you won't. You'll be gone, and this torture will be over. 'Thanks.' She hung up.

As she turned to go back to the birthing suite the sound of Suzie's moan travelled up the corridor. It had that special tone that made midwives everywhere rise from their seats with a smile.

Noni pushed open the door and grabbed the odd, banana-shaped stool from behind the curtain.

'I want to push.' Suzie and Paul greeted her with fervent relief.

'I know. It's great. Sit here, Suzie. You can hang onto these handles and bear down when you have the pain. Now that you have something to do with it, use your contractions.'

Noni put her hand on Paul's shoulder after she'd settled his wife, and steered him onto a chair behind the stool. 'Suzie can lean back into your arms.'

'I think it's coming.'

Noni pressed the nurse call buzzer once. She settled herself on a footstool in front of the birth chair and lifted Suzie's gown.

'Yep. I can see the hair. Do you want a mirror?'

'I don't want to see it but Paul wants to.'

'No worries. We'll just angle it towards him and get on with it.'

Another midwife poked her head around the corner. She met Noni's eyes and they both smiled. 'Want me?'

Noni's voice was matter-of-fact, and Suzie and Paul relaxed at the lack of tension in the room.

'Give Dr McCloud a ring and tell him now. Thanks.'

The other girl nodded. 'Will do. I'll be back.'

'Here comes another one.' Suzie strained with her body's urging and the circle of dark hair spread wider with each push.

'You're doing beautifully. Gently does it and lean back on Paul when it's done.' The muted sound of classical music and Suzie's steady breathing were the first sounds the little ears heard as the head was born.

The door opened and Iain came in quietly as the baby's shoulders rotated and with a gush the rest of the body was born. Noni lowered the little boy onto the pillow between his mother's feet.

Noni wiped the infant's mouth with a cloth and gestured for Suzie to lift her baby up.

Suzie wrenched her gown over her head to bare her skin, reached down and lifted her baby son to her chest. The baby mewled and Suzie hugged him to her breasts. 'Our baby.'

Tears ran down Paul's face as he reached around and cradled his family. 'Darling, he's beautiful.'

The cord could wait. Noni sat back. She looked up and caught Iain's eyes on her, and suddenly she felt like crying, too. It hit her then that she and this man could have shared a similar moment to this as parents. If only…

'Could you pass me one of those warm bunny rugs, please, Iain?'

When he handed it to her, Noni laid it over the baby's back and around Suzie's shoulders before sitting down again on the stool.

The umbilical cord stopped pulsating. Noni placed two clamps on either side of the area to be cut and offered the scissors. 'Would you like to cut the cord, Paul?'

He swallowed once before shaking his head.

'I would but I think I need to take a few deep breaths at the moment.'

Iain caught Noni's eye. 'Perhaps you had better do it, Sister.'

'Maybe.' Noni looked up at the mother. 'What about you, Suzie? You've done everything else.'

Suzie flicked her hair out of her face and grinned at Noni. 'Take a picture of this, someone.' She shifted the baby to her left arm and took the scissors. The thick, ropelike connection between mother and child separated with a firm snip. She handed the scissors back.

Suzie frowned suddenly and groaned. 'Hey, you said the pains would go away after I had the baby, and I've got another one.'

Noni smiled. 'You needed one more, to finish the fabulous job you've done.' A few seconds later the placenta came away and slid into the dish. Noni placed the dish on the bottom of the trolley and helped Suzie tidy herself.

Paul sighed quietly and closed his eyes.

Noni looked up. 'Can I hold Baby for a minute, Suzie?' She wrapped the rest of the bunny rug around the baby and stood quickly up and out of the way.

'Iain. Fainting father over here,' she said as Paul slid sideways off the chair onto the beanbag beside it.

Iain raised his eyebrows. 'Me?'

'Please.'

Iain sent her a level stare and then shrugged. He stepped over to the casualty.

'Sometimes it's just too much. Come on, old mate, here's a wet washcloth for your face.'

Paul opened his eyes. 'What happened?'

'It's time you went out for some fresh air. Bet you haven't eaten all day.' Iain helped him to his feet and smiled at Paul's wife.

'He'll be back in a minute. He'll be fine.'

Noni and Suzie watched Iain help Paul stagger out the door and both tried hard not to laugh.

'Poor Paul,' said Noni. They grinned at each other. 'Let's get you up on the bed and settled with this little man before he comes back.'

Soon Suzie was settled in bed with her baby nursing gently at her breast.

'I'll slip out and see if I can find Paul.'

'Before you go, Noni. Is Iain really leaving tomorrow?'

Noni stopped and met Suzie's eyes. 'Yes. Why?'

'I thought you two were an item.'

'Sometimes things don't work out, but it's not the end of the world.' She forced a smile to her face and then turned towards the door. 'I'll look for that husband of yours.'

CHAPTER ELEVEN

WHEN Noni woke early on Saturday morning she felt strangely relieved that it would soon be over. She dressed and steeled herself for one more day of pretending all was right in her world.

The first person she saw was the one she'd least wanted to see.

But this wasn't the caring doctor she'd seen for the last fortnight. He'd gone. In his place stood a hard-eyed stranger.

'Iain? What's wrong?'

'Not content with me missing the first seventeen years of Jacinta's life, are you? So how long have you two been cooking this up?' His voice was colder than she'd ever heard it, and he examined her as if she were a particularly loathsome species of insect.

The hairs on the back of her neck rose at the scent of danger and she held her answer for a moment. Her eyes darted around the room for inspiration but found nothing that cleared the mystery. 'Cooking what up?'

Just then Win came in and looked from one to the other. She sighed and crossed her arms over her ample bosom.

'Jacinta asked me if she could stay here for a while with Olivia, instead of going back to Sydney with her father.'

Noni was beginning to understand. 'And you said…?'

'The same as I said to you. I said yes.'

Iain snorted. 'Spare me. Do you think I'm going to believe you knew nothing of this, Noni?' He threw a cynical glance at both of them. 'Well, I'm leaving, as that's what you want. My sympathy goes to Harley. He has to live with you all.'

It was a very sombre crew that watched the Mercedes pull out of the driveway for the last time. Olivia started to cry on cue and Noni felt like doing the same. She draped her arm over Jacinta's shoulder and squeezed her.

'So what is all this about, missy?'

Jacinta shrugged. 'It wasn't any fun with him in Sydney before and I'm not sure what Olivia and I want to do. It is OK that I stayed, isn't it?'

Noni half laughed. 'A bit late now but, yes, it's fine. Let's go and fix your rooms properly.' She turned to her son who was staring up the empty road, and her heart sank again.

'Come on, Harley. Try and remember the good times and how much you learned while Iain was here.'

Harley turned and stared accusingly at his mother but didn't say anything. His eyes glinted with unshed tears. Then he turned and ran into the house.

Noni rubbed her temples.

Harley barely ate over the next few days. Come Wednesday morning, for once Noni was glad to leave the house and go to work before he woke up.

The shift was busy but she still had an uncomfortable feeling of disquiet all day. The afternoon clouded over and storm warnings were current on the radio in the nursery.

The first raindrops fell as she climbed onto her bike and started home, and she could smell the scent of wet grass. Harley would be soaked when he came in—she'd have a hot chocolate waiting, to warm him up.

Droplets of rain stung her arms and she ducked her head to stop them flying down her neck. It was a relief to glide in under the carport and shake the raindrops off.

The baby was crying and she walked through to the lounge, expecting to find Jacinta or at least Win tending to her.

Olivia was red-faced and sweating and Noni's disquiet turned to alarm. She scooped the baby up, soothed her and then quickly changed her soaking nappy.

'Hello? Anyone home?' She walked swiftly back into the hallway and up the stairs, and Olivia bounced on her shoulder, at peace now.

'Noni!' Aunt Win's voice floated up from downstairs, and held a thread of panic. Noni felt her own nerves tighten into real fear. Aunt Win never panicked.

'I'm here.' She descended quickly. 'What's going on?'

'Harley didn't go to school today. One of his friends just rang and asked if he was all right. He thought he must have been sick. I think Harley's run away.'

'Because Iain's gone.' Noni's head was spinning and she fought for clarity. One part wanted to throw herself on the floor and scream out her fears. The other was trying to think like a five-year-old boy and work out the most likely place to hide. The baby squirmed in her arms. 'Where's Jacinta? Why was Olivia here alone?'

'It was only for two minutes. I spoke to the bus driver and he said Harley hadn't caught the bus. Jacinta ran to the shops to see if anyone had seen him and didn't want to take Olivia out in the rain.'

As she finished speaking, Jacinta skidded to a panting, bedraggled stop at the front door.

'Nobody's seen him.' She bent over and dragged great gulps of air into her lungs. 'He has to be hiding somewhere here.'

Noni sank onto the hallway chair and the baby squirmed as she unconsciously clutched her tighter as if to keep her own child safe. She bounced up again. 'I'll check his room.'

'Here, give Olivia to me.' Win reached out and Noni blinked as her shock faded, and she handed over the child.

She ran up the stairs and Jacinta followed. They checked every cupboard, under every bed, spent longest in Iain's old room, but couldn't find Harley. Lightning flashed and the thunder rattled the windows as the rain fell in great sheets onto the roof. Noni shuddered to think of him huddled outside somewhere.

She closed her eyes but her brain was sluggish with fear. She had to get a grip and move fast. 'Think, think.' All she could think about was Harley, lost and alone, and Iain five hundred kilometres away when she needed him.

'OK. Aunt Win, phone the police and ask them to look out for him. I'll phone Iain on my mobile, grab some stuff and drive around after we've checked the garage.'

'I'll come.' Jacinta's eyes were huge in her face. 'Please, Noni.'

Noni wiped a distracted hand across her face. 'Jaz, what about Olivia?' Noni knew she had to act quickly.

'I could mind Olivia here. We'll be fine. I'd be happier if you had someone with you, Noni,' Win put in as she moved off to phone the police.

Noni was flicking through the address book for the number Iain had given her when he'd taken Harley to Sydney.

She couldn't believe Harley would have done this to her. She couldn't believe she was such a bad mother that she hadn't realised what he was going to do. She found the number and punched it in. It rang and rang and finally she heard Iain's voice.

'Iain! It's Noni.' The voice continued talking. 'Bloody answering machine.' She felt like throwing the phone against the floor and took a deep breath to regather her wits.

'Iain, if you're there, this is an emergency. Pick up the phone!'

The voice finished and the phone beeped.

'Iain, when you get home ring me on my mobile.' She gave her own number and disconnected.

Jacinta was behind her.

'He's not home.'

Win reappeared. 'The police want a photograph and will send someone around to pick it up. I'll give them the one in the frame.'

Noni thought she was going to lose her mind then. She bit her lip and fought back the nausea that clutched at her stomach. She couldn't believe this was happening. She squeezed back the tears.

'Jacinta is coming with me if you think you'll be all right with Olivia.' Her voice cracked.

'We'll be fine. I'll ring your mobile when she needs a feed. Go.'

It took five minutes to grab torches and leave. Noni barely spoke as she tried to block out images of her son, lost and frightened. The worst was the darkness and poor visibility from the storm, even though it was still only four-thirty in the afternoon.

She kept picturing Harley crouched outside in the rain, waiting for her to find him.

'Try the cricket field.' Jacinta's voice broke into her thoughts and Noni swerved to avoid a fallen branch.

Fear closed her throat again and her voice faltered. 'We have to find him soon.'

'We will. He's probably holed up somewhere warm and dry, eating his play lunch.'

'Please, God. If someone's taken him…' Her voice trailed off. 'I have to find him.' She gripped the wheel tighter. 'Why hasn't Iain phoned us?'

*   *   *

Iain was unaware of Harley's disappearance.

By the time he'd arrived in Sydney from Burra on Saturday, he'd known he was going back to Burra— for good. He'd rung Jacinta on Monday while Noni had been at work and she'd given him an ear-bashing. He smiled at the memory. She'd said she didn't know what was wrong with him. She knew what she wanted and how come he didn't? The only way he'd been able to stop her had been to tell her of his plans to return to Burra and swear her to secrecy.

The next couple of days were spent arranging the sequence of events that would be required to change his lifestyle from a Macquarie Street specialist to Burra Hospital's new obstetrician. Dr Soams had arranged an interview with the hospital for Friday, but it was a formality.

He needed to ring Noni. But he hated the thought she would be so far away when he spoke to her. In the end he accepted that he would be seeing her very soon.

It was over. Tonight he'd cleaned out his office. Tomorrow he was out of here. He threw his bag on the lounge and strolled over to the answering machine. His finger pressed the button and the urgency in Noni's voice rose to meet him. Undercurrents he'd never heard before lifted the hair on the back of his neck. He reached for the handset and dialled Win's number.

The beep, beep, beep of the engaged signal teased him and he stabbed the cut-off. He tried Noni's mobile number. It was out of range. Iain slammed the phone down and stared out the window. He had a bad feeling about this.

Noni and Jacinta passed two police patrols as they turned for home. It was useless. The rain continued to fall as if it was auditioning for Noah's ark and the mobile phone was dead. It had been dark for a couple of hours. She'd have to go home. It was nine o'clock.

The fear rose like a monster in her throat as her headlights reflected the volume of water rushing through drains and gutters. Surely he wouldn't hide in a stormwater drain?

'Aunt Win might have news.' She spoke to Jacinta as the ute rolled to a stop but she was really trying to reassure herself. At home, one look at the older woman's face conveyed the lack of progress in the search. She had even more bad news.

'The local radio is alerting everyone to the search and state emergency workers are dividing the swampland into a grid for a foot patrol.'

Car headlights shone into the driveway and pulled into the garage. They all turned to look and Noni felt the tears well up.

'It's Iain!' Noni was out of the door and into his arms before the car had barely enough time to stop.

He squeezed her tight and she burst into tears from the fears and trauma of the day. It was the last thing she wanted to do but couldn't help herself.

'Hey. It's OK, darling. Settle down.'

Noni pulled herself back off his chest and wiped her nose with the back of her hand. She sniffed and caught her breath. 'It's Harley, Iain. He's gone. He's run away.'

Iain's face drained of colour and he squeezed her shoulders. 'Come inside. How long has he been missing?'

'Since this morning. We didn't know who to call when we couldn't reach you. Jacinta couldn't remember the surname of your housekeeper.' She was tripping over words, trying to tell him everything at once as he ushered them back towards the house.

'Slow down, darling.'

Noni turned around to look at him, confused by the loving inflection in his voice.

He realised she was in no fit state to understand. 'It's OK. We'll talk about it all later. Just know that I'll do anything you need to get Harley back.'

Her brain refused to think about it so she said, 'Thank you for coming, Iain.'

She took another steadying breath. 'I've driven and looked everywhere. The police and volunteers are out looking for him. They think he might be on the swampland. Why haven't they found him?' Her voice trailed off.

She sank back into the lounge and shut her eyes. Harley had been on his own for hours. She shuddered.

'Aunt Win's made sandwiches. Please, have one.' Jacinta's eyes were huge in her face.

Noni waved them away. 'I couldn't eat anything. He must be hungry and cold, Jaz. I don't think I can sit here all night, waiting for the phone to ring.'

Jacinta looked grim. 'Try to eat something.'

After Noni nodded distractedly, Jacinta slipped out

of the lounge, surreptitiously picking up Iain's car keys from the coffee table as she did so.

A few minutes later there was a knock on the door and they all looked up. Noni put her hand to her throat and Iain strode across to answer it.

It was the police. No luck. Could Noni think of anywhere else that he could have gone? After the police had left there was little to say.

Win stuck her head around the door. 'Anyone seen Jacinta?'

Iain looked up. 'She was here a minute ago— maybe she's gone to bed.'

'No, I checked. I think she's gone out to search for Harley.'

Iain looked on the coffee table for his car keys, then groaned in frustration. 'Why didn't she tell us what she was going to do?'

Noni stood up and turned to face him. 'That's right, Iain. And we would have said, ''Go for it, Jacinta.''? She knew we would try to stop her. Don't underestimate your daughter, Iain. I don't.' She ran her hand through her hair.

'I'm terrified for Harley and I'm not happy about Jacinta being out alone at night either. But if she's had an idea, I believe she's trying to do what she thinks will help. She's more streetwise than I am and I admire that in her. I'll take her help if it brings my son back.'

Iain glanced at his watch. 'Well, I'm not sure I like the idea of my daughter being streetwise, but she's probably slept in more unusual places than we could think of.' He took a deep breath and straightened his shoulders. 'And I'm proud of her, looking for Harley. I just wish I'd been there to look for her when she needed me.'

Noni felt the tears prick her eyes. 'I think we both need a hug.'

'Come here.' Iain held open his arms and Noni stepped into them. She sighed and closed her eyes.

'I'm so scared.'

He enfolded her and she drew energy from him until she felt she could go on again.

The night dragged on and Noni stared at the phone, willing it to ring.

At a quarter to eleven it wasn't the phone that rang but the doorbell. Noni stumbled to fling it open and Iain was right behind her.

Harley stood there. His cheeks were scratched and his shirt was soaked and torn, but he was alive.

'Mummy,' he said, and burst into tears.

Jacinta stood behind him with a huge grin on her face.

Noni scooped him up and hugged him fiercely to her body. His little arms clung to her neck in a stranglehold. She put her other arm out and drew Jacinta into the hug. 'Where was he?'

'Asleep under a bench at the railway station. I've slept under them heaps of times. The good news is he didn't know how to catch the train to Sydney.'

Iain and Win made all the phone calls and Noni sat with Harley asleep in her lap. The tears had dried on her face and her world was slowly righting itself.

Jacinta had been thanked so many times she had uttered 'Spare me' and gone to feed her baby.

'Why don't you go to bed, Noni?' Iain came up behind the lounge chair and massaged her neck.

She rolled her shoulders under his hands, moved her head from side to side and sighed with bliss. She'd always known he had beautiful hands.

'I'll never sleep but I will have to move. My legs have gone numb under Harley.'

'Here. Let me lift him. Would you like to sleep with him tonight in your bed?'

'Put him in his room. I'll hear him if he wants me. I need you tonight, Iain. He won't mind me sleeping with you—that is, if you don't.'

Iain laughed softly, dropped a tender kiss on her lips and lifted the boy easily out of her lap to carry him up the stairs.

CHAPTER TWELVE

HALF an hour later Noni had showered and was sipping the hot chocolate Iain had insisted she needed.

He came back into the room, sat down and slid his arm around her. 'This wasn't quite the situation and setting I'd planned but I do have something to say.'

Noni put the cup down and tried to calm the sudden thumping in her heart. She looked into the face of the man she'd come to love and finally realised she had to stay with him despite the risks.

'First of all, I'm sorry for accusing you of knowing Jacinta was planning on staying with you. On Saturday, it took me until about fifty kilometres south of Burra to realise that you hadn't known Jacinta was going to stay behind. I think I always knew you'd never stoop to underhand methods to arrange that change of plan. It would have been Jacinta's idea, although for the life of me I couldn't understand why she left telling me until the last minute.' He grimaced and squeezed her shoulder. 'I was so disappointed in her lack of loyalty I blamed you. I'm sorry.'

Noni ran her finger along his jaw. 'I understand that. Before she went to bed, Jacinta said she only wanted to make sure we still saw each other. That she could see we were good for each other if we could hang in there. She stayed so we would still keep in contact.'

'She's a stubborn woman.'

'Just like her father.' Noni took a deep breath and hoped the offer was still open. 'But I can see what she means. I will take you on your terms. I think we should try to make a life together, and it's no good Harley and I staying in Burra if our hearts are down in Sydney with you.' She expelled her breath. There. She'd said it and she meant it.

He took her face in his hands and kissed her gently.

'Ah Noni. You're too much for me. Thank you for your typically brave offer, but let me finish. Where was I? Oh, yes. My stubborn daughter. I am *not* stubborn, by the way! It only took another five kilometres to realise I didn't want to leave Burra either. The challenges of a country practice might be the answer to rejuvenating my interest in obstetrics. But it's you, not the town, which is drawing me back. If you'll have me.'

Noni was lost now. 'What are you saying, Iain?'

'I'm saying…I love you. I want to marry you. I want to live with you, in Burra if you want to, for the rest of our lives.' He took her hand in his and kissed her fingers.

'Say that again,' Noni whispered. She couldn't believe it.

'I love you. I love the way you stand up to me despite the fact you only come up to the top button of my shirt. I love your empathy with the pregnant mums and fathers-to-be and your huge well of love for Harley. I love your kindness and non-judgemental attitude with Jacinta that's helped bridge a gap between my daughter and myself, and I thought that could never be.' He kissed her again.

Noni couldn't believe it. Today had been the worst day of her life yet it had ended so wonderfully she thought she almost couldn't take in such extremes of emotion. 'Why didn't you ring me and tell me you were coming back?'

'I rang Jacinta on Monday, and she blasted me for leaving. I wanted to talk to you but can't stand the phone. I hated the thought of five hundred kilometres between us while we spoke.'

She remembered the last time he'd gone to Sydney when he'd said the same thing. She supposed she could forgive him. 'I'll have to set you up with e-mail if you ever go away. I can't stand *not* hearing from you.'

He laughed. 'I had hoped distance would make your heart grow fonder by the time I arrived back and planned to explain it all then.'

'Well, *do not* do it again. We'll make a contingency plan.' She couldn't believe how good it was to be back talking to Iain like this again.

'I'm sorry. I wanted everything under control before I came back.'

'I'm going to call you the Control Master. Please, stop trying to control everything!'

'I'll never control you. Can we go back to you being my teacher? For ever!'

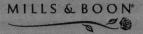

FREE

4 BOOKS

AND A SURPRISE GIFT!

We would like to take this opportunity to thank you for reading this Mills & Boon® book by offering you the chance to take FOUR more specially selected titles from the Medical Romance™ series absolutely FREE! We're also making this offer to introduce you to the benefits of the Reader Service™—

- ★ FREE home delivery
- ★ FREE monthly Newsletter
- ★ FREE gifts and competitions
- ★ Exclusive Reader Service discounts
- ★ Books available before they're in the shops

Accepting these FREE books and gift places you under no obligation to buy; you may cancel at any time, even after receiving your free shipment. Simply complete your details below and return the entire page to the address below. *You don't even need a stamp!*

YES! Please send me 4 free Medical Romance books and a surprise gift. I understand that unless you hear from me, I will receive 6 superb new titles every month for just £2.49 each, postage and packing free. I am under no obligation to purchase any books and may cancel my subscription at any time. The free books and gift will be mine to keep in any case.

MIZEC

Ms/Mrs/Miss/Mr ....Initials ....
BLOCK CAPITALS PLEASE

Surname ....

Address ....

....

....Postcode ....

Send this whole page to:
UK: FREEPOST CN81, Croydon, CR9 3WZ
EIRE: PO Box 4546, Kilcock, County Kildare (stamp required)